From a young age, N[...]
up and writing storie[...]
on hold. Nyrae worke[...]
fell in love and marri[...]
high school. In 2004[...]
new baby girl made a move from Oregon to Southern
California and that's when everything changed. As a
stay-at-home mom for the first time, her passion for
writing flared to life again. She hasn't stopped writing
since. With two incredible daughters, an awesome
husband and her days spent writing what she loves,
Nyrae considers herself the luckiest girl in the world.
She still resides in sunny Southern California, where
she loves spending time with her family and sneaking
away to the bookstore with her laptop. Nyrae Dawn
also writes adult romance under the name Kelley
Vitollo.

To find out more about Nyrae Dawn, visit
www.nyraedawn.com. Find her on Facebook at
nyraedawnwrites and follow her on Twitter
@NyraeDawn.

ALSO BY NYRAE DAWN AND
PUBLISHED BY HEADLINE ETERNAL

THE GAMES TRILOGY
Charade
Façade

What a Boy Wants
What a Boy Needs

Nyrae Dawn

CHARADE

headline
ETERNAL

First published in Great Britain in 2013 by HEADLINE ETERNAL
An imprint of HEADLINE PUBLISHING GROUP

1

Cataloguing in Publication Data is available from the British Library

ISBN 978 1 4722 0878 1

Typeset in Electra by Palimpsest Book Production Limited,
Falkirk, Stirlingshire

Printed and bound by CPI Group
(UK) Ltd, Croydon, CR0 4YY

Headline's policy is to use papers that are natural, renewable
and recyclable products and made from wood grown in sustainable
forests. The logging and manufacturing processes are expected to
conform to the environmental regulations of the country of origin.

HEADLINE PUBLISHING GROUP
An Hachette UK Company
338 Euston Road
London NW1 3BH

www.eternalromancebooks.co.uk
www.headline.co.uk
www.hachette.co.uk

To Tara. Just because you're my BFF and BFFs should always have a book dedicated to them. Love ya and thanks for being part of my life.

ACKNOWLEDGEMENTS

As always, huge thanks to my wonderful hubby and awesome girls. I know you hear a lot of 'just one more minute' and it turns out to be fifteen. Thanks for understanding and for all your support.

Mom for always believing in me.

My mother-in-law for being probably the best mother-in-law in the world and for your love of spending time with your grandkids.

To my beta readers who gave their time to Colt, Cheyenne and myself: Wendy Higgins, Jolene Perry, Kristy Z, Morgan Shamy, Allie B, Cassie Mae and Jessica Skondin.

Also a thanks to Kelly Smith.

Steph Campbell for being awesome and for the hours you were willing to spend drinking coffee with me while I vented about everything under the sun. I miss you hard. When are we planning that writing retreat again?

Sebastian Hawkins. Maybe it's silly to thank one of my characters, but you started this journey of boy

POV for me and you will always hold a special place in my heart for it. Colt is better because of you.

My readers. This has been such an incredible journey and I have you to thank for it.

HUGE thanks to anyone I might have missed.

CHAPTER ONE

CHEYENNE

I stare, unable to take my eyes off the scene in front of me as I try to process what my boyfriend just said.

"How exactly is being naked in bed with another girl not what it looks like?" My voice comes out completely smooth even though my stomach is a mess. It's dropped to my feet and I feel like I could throw up at any second.

Please don't let me throw up in front of them.

I look at him, in bed next to some redhead and all Gregory can do is stare back. This is the guy I'd stupidly allowed myself to begin to trust after so long together — against my better judgment since I know, I've *always* known you can never really depend on someone.

Panic threatens me. Like the burned edge of a paper, flames threatening to take me over. My heart speeds up. My chest hurts. My vision starts to blur.

No. I cannot have a panic attack right now. I haven't had one in years and I refuse to let this bastard get the best of me. But still, my body's trying not to listen.

My hands curl, opening and closing into fists. It's like a flood of energy sent to every part of me, sending me into overdrive.

With everything inside me, I fight to stamp it down.

"Cheyenne, baby . . . I'm sorry," Gregory says.

I shake my head back and forth, take a step back, more pissed and petrified than I've been in so long. He jumps out of bed. Naked.

"You know I love you. It was so hard last year . . ." He's reaching for his boxers, tugging them on while he talks and moves toward me. "When you were still in high school and I was here. I just missed you so much, but this was the last time. I told her this was the last time." He glances at her like he wants her to verify this fact, but she just scowls at him and starts to yank on her clothes. Gregory looks back at me. "I screwed up, but you know you're the only one I love."

Nausea hits me again. Lies.

"You missed me so you screwed some other girl?"

Red huffs, but we both ignore her.

"I'm a guy, Chey . . ." He shakes his head as if I'm being unreasonable for making a big deal of a little mistake.

"You're a *guy?* That's the worst excuse I've ever heard. We were together all summer at home, and we've been here at college two weeks already, and you're still screwing her? That makes perfect sense! And yeah . . . thanks for not making me ask how long it's been going on. A smarter man might have waited to see if I assumed this was the first time."

Gregory's eyes stretch wide as he realizes his mistake. *Never admit more than you have to.* With his attorney parents, he should know that. Jackass.

My eyes sting, but there's no way I'm giving either of them the satisfaction of tears. I stopped giving people the satisfaction of knowing how they affect me a long time ago.

Red stands and glares at me, bumping Gregory's shoulder as she passes him, saying, "I'm outta here."

"Wait," I say, recognizing her. "Didn't you introduce me to her at the welcome party two nights ago?"

Red has the nerve to blush at this before she stomps out. She definitely has no right to toss any evil glares in my direction considering she knew Gregory has a girlfriend. Had. The word leaves a bad taste in my mouth. He was supposed to be safe. Our families are friends. He treated me so good when we were together. What is it about me that makes people think they can take advantage and toss me aside? Why am I so easy to betray?

A wave of dizziness hits me as I think about my mom. I try to shake the thoughts from my head. I've worked so hard not to be that girl—the girl whose own mother couldn't love her enough to stay around. This isn't the way my life is supposed to go. Not anymore. Everything's been perfect for the past ten years. I'm a new person now and things were supposed to keep getting better. An easy, simple, perfect life to make up for what I didn't have before.

I'm Cheyenne Marshall. The captain of the dance team. Voted most popular girl in my high school. I have friends. Tons of them.

But that was then . . . in high school. And now I'm here with Gregory in his territory where I have no friends yet. Every single person I know here, I know through him. I close my eyes and reach out a hand to steady myself against the wall as the reality of my new life slams down. I'm stuck here. Alone.

No, no, no. I can't cry. Can't lose it. I'm going to lose it.

The muscles in my fingers tense, trying to curl again.

"Chey . . . come on, baby. You know I love you. We belong together." He steps toward me and there's a second—one second where I consider holding my hand out to his. This is Gregory. I lost my virginity to him. I planned to marry him, because we fit. He wouldn't leave me. I worked hard to be the kind of girl people don't walk away from. I . . . oh God. I trusted him. How could I have let myself trust someone?

He's been screwing other girls! I can't look past that.

I fight back the tears smashing against the dam of my eyelids. "No, Gregory. We don't belong together."

He stands between the bed and me, his boxers all crooked, looking very . . . shall we say, deflated? "What are you saying, Chey? You want to break up?" He huffs a frustrated laugh. "That's a crap idea. You don't even know anybody here. None of the guys are going to go after you. They know you're mine."

His ego makes me nauseous. I won't be *that* girl. Won't be alone, and need him like he thinks.

"I am not yours."

"Chey . . ." He's trying to sound all gentle. "I'm just saying that's how they'll always see you."

"Not everyone," I say, trying to smirk. Trying to show him I don't need him.

His face hardens and his eyes slant.

"Who? Someone's been hitting on you?"

The pissed off look on his face fuels me.

"That's none of your business," I say, crossing my arms. "All you need to know is, while we were together I never cheated. But we're not together anymore." Let him suffer with that thought the way I'll suffer with the images of him and Red in bed naked together. I turn to leave.

"Cheyenne!" he calls after me, but I keep going, slamming the door to his apartment. I don't drive very far before pulling off to the side of the road. In the safety of my car, I give myself five minutes to let go. Five minutes for the loud sobs to wrack my body.

How could I have given him power over me? Any

power? Gregory was supposed to be my normal. Constant. He wasn't supposed to leave me. More tears. My head drops forward against the steering wheel. All the pain inside me wells up, sloughing up old dirt I haven't let myself think about for so long.

"Baby, Mommy, will be right back, okay? You stay in this room till I come back."

Mama kisses my forehead and walks out of the room. It's loud. So loud with the music and the banging that I put my hands over my ears. She said she wouldn't leave me. That she'd never leave me alone again.

I huddle in the corner, my knees pulled up to my chest and my hands still on my ears and my eyes squeezed closed. She'll be right back. She promised. The door pushes open and I don't know how I know, but I do. I let out a breath, knowing it has to be her. My eyes jerk open. A guy, a big guy with a beard comes in and a woman too. They're kissing and it's gross. Their hands are all over each other. What are they doing?

"Vince. There's a kid in the corner." For a second I wonder if they'll help me. If they'll find my mama for me, but then they both start to laugh. My eyes are stinging and tears slide down my cheeks.

"Get out of here, kid! You don't wanna see this." The scary man yells. He's right. I just want Mama. I want to go home.

I push to my feet and run out of the room. There

are people everywhere. So many people I can hardly get through. They push me and step on me and the music is so loud it makes my heart pound.

I keep searching through the house. Searching for people. For Mama. The house stinks, but I don't know what the smell is. Someone spills a drink on me and I cry harder. This smell I know. It's beer. Mama's old boyfriend used to like to drink it.

No one offers to help me.

I can't find Mama.

She left me alone.

Another voice. Another man . . . "I'll help you find your mama . . ."

Sitting up, I shudder and wipe the tears away. I'm not that kid anymore. I don't want to be defined by those memories. I try to focus on the here and now.

I might not have completely let Gregory into my heart like normal girlfriends do, but I trusted him more than I should have. I vow to myself right then and there I will never make that mistake again. People hurt you if you let them. I won't be hurt again.

With a glance in the mirror I see that I look halfway decent. There's only a light pink tinge to my dark brown eyes. No red blotches mark my clear skin. Opening my purse, I pull out my eyeliner and reapply. Mascara comes next. I even add a little lip gloss. Still looking in the mirror I reiterate, "I'm not that kid anymore."

That quickly, I'm Cheyenne Marshall again. Not the little girl at that party—the girl who gets abandoned and panics. I'm stronger than that. I'm the Cheyenne Marshall I fought to become.

One deep breath later, I start the car again and drive away.

"Men are such assholes. My last boyfriend cheated on me, too. Things are so much easier with Veronica."

My eyes snap over to my dorm-mate. School's only been in a couple weeks and we're never here at the same time. This is probably only the third time I've spoken with her. "How—"

"I'm bisexual," Andrea sits up on her bed. "Problem with it?" Her pink hair is tied back in a ponytail and she's wearing a pink volleyball shirt.

I've never known someone who likes both girls and guys before. I don't know why, but I would expect her to look different.

I stop studying her when her question sinks in. I straighten up as though that will make me less transparent. One look at me and she knew about Gregory. "No. I was going to say how did you know my boyfriend cheated on me?" See how nonchalantly I said that? It's because I don't care.

I need her to think I don't care.

Without waiting for her to reply, I turn over, facing the wall as I settle on my bed. The last thing I want is for her to see I really am upset. How embarrassing is this? My first two weeks in college and I find out my boyfriend is sleeping with other people. Or at least one other person.

How did this happen to me?

"Hiding in your bed isn't going to make it go away."

"I'm not hiding," I tell her without moving.

"He's not worth it. Don't let him get you upset."

How does she know what Gregory is worth? That isn't what I say because I'm not supposed to be upset. Not over a guy. I'm better than that. "Please. Like I'd let him hurt me. I'm over it. Just tired, Andrea."

She shuffles behind me and I'm pretty sure she stood up. "Sure you are. And the name is Andy."

The door creaks open and then slams closed. My heart jumps at that sound. Who does that girl think she is? Pretending to know me when she doesn't have a clue who I am. I bounce back. Move forward. Forget the past where people leave me behind. I'm definitely not going to let Gregory and Red get me down.

Which is exactly why I should get out of this bed right now and move on. Find that guy I lied about or go to a party. Do something. I'm in college and nothing should have me lying in this bed.

But I'm tired. Too tired to do anything, so instead of getting up, I pull a blanket over my head and try to figure out what happened to my life.

*   *   *

"You sound tired," Aunt Lily says through the phone.

"Do I? I'm not sure why. Everything's fine." I swing my legs off the side of the bed and sit up. The second I push my dark hair behind my ear, it flops free again.

Aunt Lily sighs. "If you're sure." For just a second I wish she'd push. Wonder if I could tell her, but that means letting her in. I don't need to be pushed.

I stand. There's no reason for me to still be in bed. It happened, nothing will fix it, so I might as well get over it. There's no point in dwelling on facts. Not when they'll be there no matter what I do.

And there's also no point in holding off on this. Aunt Lily and Uncle Mark will find out. It's better if it comes from me. "Gregory . . . he cheated on me." The words make me fall back to the bed. Saying them makes it more real. He cheated on me. I played the perfect game. The perfect girlfriend and it still wasn't enough.

Lily sucks in a breath. "You're sure?"

"I came back to campus early and I found them together."

There's a few seconds of silence on the line. "I'm so sorry, sweetie."

I hear the pity in her voice. Know exactly what she's thinking. After all she's been through, she shouldn't have to deal with this, too. I don't want pity. "I'm fine, Lily. It's really not a big deal. I was thinking of breaking up with him anyway." The lie rolls easily off my tongue.

She pauses and I wonder if she wants more from me. Wishes I could let myself be closer to her. Really let her in. For a second, I let myself wish it too.

"It still can't be easy. Are you sure? You never let anything get you down, Cheyenne. It has to hurt."

All over again, I feel like I might vomit. My head pounds. Stop it! I'm past panicking. I don't let myself freak out anymore. "It happens, Lily. I'm shocked, but they say most young relationships don't work, right?" I play the game, hoping she buys it.

Aunt Lily sighs. "I'm proud of you . . . Your mom would be too," she adds.

With that my body tenses. Would she? I don't know. The woman I knew doesn't seem to be the same one Lily grew up with. The one I knew left me alone at drunken parties and didn't care if I went to school or not. A flash of Mom's smile jumps into my head and makes my heart hurt. I loved her smile. Loved her laugh.

My eyes sting again. "Someone's at my door. I need to go," I lie and hang up.

I fight for renewed strength to push through me. I won't be that little girl again. I don't need Gregory. Anyone. I'll show him I can move forward. I'm better off without him. If there's one thing I know, there's no way in hell I'll risk getting close to someone again.

CHAPTER TWO

COLT

Dying people have a distinct smell to them. Even people who could have months to go. It's an almost old smell that clings to their skin. Which is gross as hell, but when it's someone you love, you don't think about how disgusting it is, but how much it fucking sucks.

The second I walk into the apartment, the scent hits me. I'm not sure whether to breathe through my nose and risk catching another whiff or through my mouth and puke, which makes me about the biggest pussy on the planet. If she can take going through it, I should be able to visit.

"Colton? Is that you?" Her voice sounds happy despite what she's going through. Does she smell the death like I do? Does it make her nauseous or is she immune? *I'm such a prick.*

"Of course it is, Mom. You expecting some other gorgeous, young guy to show up?" I round the corner into her living room. The curtains are open in the big window on the wall. She's always loved sunshine.

I wonder what the hell there is to be so sun-shiny about.

Mom laughs as she's sitting in her old-tattered wheelchair. The robe I bought her for Christmas like eight years ago is around her shoulders. It has holes in it. The stupid thing needed to be thrown away a long time ago, but she doesn't throw anything away. When you don't have much, you take care of the stuff you do have.

I lean forward and kiss her forehead. I feel like a dick because I have to hold my breath to do it. She's not wearing a hat today and all that's left of her hair is fuzz. "What's up?" Dust kicks up when I fall into the chair beside her.

"Not much. How are you today?" Her voice cracks and she starts to cough. Damn if I don't want to plug my ears so I don't have to hear it. Yeah. What a good son I am. She'd do anything for me, but I can hardly stand looking at her.

"How are you feelin'?" It's a much more important question than anything about me.

Her hair used to be blonde and shiny. I remember people saying it looked like sunshine. Maybe that's why she likes the curtains open so much. Winter will be hard. *She probably won't be here* . . .

"I feel great." Mom crosses her arms.

I roll my eyes. Yeah. How great can she feel? She's dying. The docs say it could be a week, could be three months. You never can tell with this stuff. That's a shitty answer if you ask me. They're doctors. Aren't they supposed to know that? If they can tell you you're going to die, they should be able to narrow it down a little better.

"Mom . . ."

"Colton," she throws back at me, a smile tilting her lips. "Tell me about school. How are your classes?"

Shitty. I hate them. They're not nearly as impor-tant as what's going on with you. "They're cool. It's only been a couple weeks." Every year it's the same. It's all she cares about and all she talks about and every time I feel like I want to explode. I shouldn't be worried about grades. I should be taking care of her—doing whatever the hell it takes to take care of her. It's why I do the things I do.

Mom gives me another smile, her eyes a mixture of joy and pain. That look has the power to eat me up inside, like it burns through me the same way the cancer is burning through her body, destroying everything in sight. She touches my leg. Jesus, her fingers are thin.

"I can't believe my son is a junior in college. You've grown into a man so quickly. I always knew you could do anything, Colton."

Now guilt is my disease. Because I don't see the point. Because I never gave a shit about going to college. I know who I am and what I amount to and no stupid degree will change that. Her? She always wanted it for me. She was born a crack baby, and survived. Bounced around between foster homes and survived. She always knew who her mom was— high school drop-out, runaway, drug addict. Mom didn't do drugs, but she got pregnant with me young, just like her mom did. Became a high school drop-out. Are we seeing a pattern here?

The shitty part is my money comes from the thing that's caused her all her problems. Drugs.

She's survived everything. Not let it get her down. Worked her ass off. Took my dickhead dad in when he stumbled back into our lives and tried to be my mom and dad when he was gone.

All she ever wanted was for me to finish high school. Go to college, like that bullshit would make me better than my destiny.

"It's not that big a deal, Mom." I squeeze her hand so she doesn't see I'm pissed, but do it carefully so I don't hurt her.

"Yes, it is."

She got sick when I was a senior in high school and it happened fast. I promised her if she got better, I'd do everything she wanted. I'd go to school. We applied for scholarships, financial aid and all that together and she did start to get better. We thought she beat more odds, but by then, I was stuck. I'd made a promise and I knew it meant more to her than her life.

Three years later, I'm still in school and she's really dying this time. All she wants is to know I'm going to finish—like the piece of paper will all make it worth it, or something.

"What time's Maggie coming home?" A subject change is definitely in order. Maggie's an ex-nurse Mom became friends with. They're roommates and she's Mom's caregiver now. Hospice comes in to check on her, but it helps knowing Maggie's here all the time. We struggled for insurance all our lives, but once you're dying, things are different. Sucks that it has to come to that.

"About an hour. I'm really tired though." She yawns. It happens like that a lot. She'll seem okay, but then her body can hardly stay awake any longer.

"I'll put you to bed."

"I'm okay. I want to visit with you."

"It's okay. I need to go to work anyway. I just wanted to stop in and see how you're doing." At my fake job. Fast food won't bring in the kind of money and flexibility I need to be here for her. Hospice might take care of the fact that she's dying, but that's not all there is to worry about.

"If you're sure." She yawns again. I stand, about to push her into the other room, but she stops me. "I feel like walking. Can you help me walk?"

I squeeze my eyes shut, pain lancing through me. How fucked up is this? She's thirty-eight years old.

She shouldn't need my help walking to her bedroom. "Absolutely."

She leans on me as I help lift her from the chair. Her arm wraps around me loosely, so I hold her tight to make sure she doesn't fall. It takes four minutes to make a thirty second walk, but soon we make it to her bedroom. To the hospital bed in her room. I help her sit down, but when I try to take the robe off, she stops me. "I like to wear it. It makes me feel close to you."

I bite my tongue. Shit, this is hard. "That's what all the ladies say." I wink at her before making sure she can lay down okay. Pulling the covers up, I give her another kiss on the head. "I'll call you later, okay?"

She doesn't answer and I know it's because she's worn out. My hands are begging to hit something. To do something, anything to try and make the pain inside go away.

When I get to her bedroom door, I hear a creaked, "Colton?"

Turing back, I look at her. "You can do anything in the world. I've always known that. Don't forget it."

My insides shatter. I'm definitely not who she thinks I am and I'm not even sure I want to be. Luckily, I don't have to answer her, because that quickly, she's out.

There's a different smell permeating the next house

I walk into: alcohol, weed, and who knows what else. Music thumps so loud the walls vibrate.

"'Sup, man?" Adrian nods his head at me. He's leaning against the wall with a girl kissing his neck.

"Havin' fun?" I smile at him, knowing he's not going to be in the living room with this chick much longer. They'll find a room, closet, car or something soon. Not that I blame him.

"You know it," Adrian replies and I keep walking.

When I left home, all I wanted was to be alone, but stepping into our packed, shitty, little house I know this is exactly what I need. Distraction. Probably the same kind Adrian's getting.

I head straight for my secret stash, locked in my closet, grab the bottle of Tequila and take it with me. Space opens up on the couch as soon as I walk back into the room, so I take it, putting the bottle to my lips and gulping some down at the same time.

It isn't two minutes later I feel someone sit beside me. "Hey, Colt."

Still leaning against the back of the couch, I turn my head to look at Deena. I knew it would be her. Her black hair's pulled back. She's wearing all kinds of makeup, but I don't care about any of that. She's exactly what I want right now.

"Wha'cha doin'?" I ask.

"Looking for you." She pulls her bottom lip into

her mouth and I know it's a game. I'm okay with it being one too. I wouldn't have it any other way.

"Then what are you doing way over there?" I don't move. Don't have to.

Deena doesn't have to be asked twice. She climbs onto my lap and her mouth comes down on mine. Screw the tequila. Screw everything else. I grab her, taking the kiss over and fighting to forget everything else.

It doesn't work, but I find a way to pretend.

CHAPTER THREE

CHEYENNE

I can't believe how much it sucks to walk across campus alone. I feel like a loser, like everyone knows, even though they probably don't. *Yet.* The school's not that huge, so it's bound to get around soon.

My phone buzzes. Seeing it's Gregory for the ten millionth time, I hit ignore. Does he really think I'm going to talk to him? That after one day I'm ready to hear more of his excuses? Obviously he doesn't know me at all. Did I ever give him a chance to really know me?

I have a sudden huge craving for caffeine. Nothing makes things better like an iced, skinny caramel macchiato. I pick up my phone to call someone and realize I have no one to go get coffee with me. No one. I haven't really had the chance to get to know many of the girls here. The ones I do know are the people Gregory introduced me to—girls in his sister's sorority and girlfriends of his frat brothers. I can't believe I was stupid enough to let this happen to me.

My heart starts to beat faster. I breathe deep to try and calm it.

It doesn't take long to get to the coffee house and order. I sit in the corner, trying to work through my mess of a life. Gregory's words bounce around in my brain. *No one's going to go after you. They know you're mine.*

I hate that he's right. Need him to be wrong.

How the hell do I do that alone though? Ugh. I don't want to date. Just the thought of the smiley, get-to-know-you phase makes me want to puke. And dating here at school isn't going to be easy, considering everyone seems to be friends with Gregory, or at least know who he is.

Gregory.

A moment of hurt sneaks its way into my heart. I don't want to miss the idea of him. The idea wasn't real. I don't even know if I loved Gregory. Yeah, we said it, but did I really love him? Love, on principle, scares the hell out of me. I haven't let myself love someone in . . .

"You can't go where Mommy's going."

I squeeze my eyes shut as though that will quiet Mom's voice in my brain.

I might not have loved Gregory, but I thought we would be together forever. I thought we'd be happy together. Now, I know I wasn't the only one with secrets. At least mine didn't consist of being with someone else.

And why does every thought in my brain have to

go back to Gregory? I'm a nineteen-year-old college girl. I should be living it up. Enjoying my independence and . . . singleness.

I sit up straighter. I might feel like crap inside, but I'm not about to show it.

I look around. None of the guys who walk in the coffee shop are Cheyenne material. And why am I looking at guys anyway? *Because I made it look like someone's been hitting on me. Or maybe I just want to show him that people will look at me.*

The door opens. Oh my God. I duck down in my seat. What are you doing, Cheyenne. Sit tall, be proud. You're better than this.

Only I can't make myself do it.

I gave him two years and he doesn't care?

He called me half an hour ago yet here he is with Red on his arm.

Two years.

Oh God. My chest hurts. My breaths come out faster and my vision becomes blurry.

This can't be happening to me.

I fight to slow my breathing—find something to concentrate on, keeping my eyes anywhere except on Gregory. There's a little menu with their specials and I read it—the same thing over and over just to give myself something to focus on. The coffee shop gets kind of quiet. An eerie feeling settles over me, and I swear I hear whispers.

I look up, hating myself for not having more self-control. I immediately wish I hadn't peeked.

I glance over again, see Gregory say something to Red, kiss her and then run outside. I'm pretty sure Gregory didn't see me, but the fact that Red is walking over tells me she did. It's strange, the conflicting emotions warring inside me. There's the tough Chey. The one I've worked to become who wants to get up and give her hell, but the weak girl—the one who hid in rooms at the parties and cried when Mom was gone – just wants to freak out.

"He feels sorry for you, you know?" Red crosses her arms.

"And I feel sorry for you, if you believe that." I roll my eyes at her.

"We've been together since last year. I knew about you. I also know your families are friends. That Gregory took you under his wing, and now he feels some stupid sense of obligation to you. That's all it is. I know it. He knows it and now you know it too."

Her words hit all of my buttons. I feel used. I was an obligation to Mom, then to Lily and Mark, and now Gregory too? And with him, he doesn't even know everything about me. *No!* "Did you ever think he said that to get in your pants? I mean, not that it was obviously very hard for him to get there."

Her face turns as red as her hair. "Screw you. I feel sorry for you, thinking all this time he really still wanted to be with you. I know what it really is. He wants me. Now you can live with that. If you'll excuse me, my boyfriend should be back any second. He just went to get something out of the car."

She turns and walks away. I push to get up and find a way to defend myself, but Gregory's voice breaks through. He's standing by the door, obviously having walked back in.

"Watch where you're going!" Gregory says.

Gregory's standing straight, trying to make himself look tall and Red steps up to his side. Another guy stands in front of him. He has dark blond, clouds-over-sunset colored hair. It's messy, like he hasn't combed it all day and he's a good four inches taller than Gregory. His pants are wrinkled and there's a hole in the knee. I can tell it's from wear and not jeans that you buy to look like that.

A black t-shirt stretches across his chest and all the way down his right arm are tattoos. Like, so many of them I can't even see his skin.

Tattoo Guy laughs. I see the tightness in Gregory's face. I wonder if Red knows it. If she knows him well enough to read what his look is saying. He's pissed that this guy would laugh at him, and embarrassed, too.

Tattoo Guy turns away, shaking his head, but Gregory grabs his arm. He doesn't like to be made a fool of and I'm sure he needs to show off for his new girl. Not smart. I've never known Gregory to get in a fight and this guy looks like he does it often.

"I'm thinking you want to let go of my arm now, Pretty Boy." Tattoo Guy doesn't jerk his arm back, though I'm sure he could. He just stares at Gregory. My boyfriend—no, ex-boyfriend—returns the stare for a few seconds. Something is passing between them, and I want to know what it is.

"Whatever." Gregory's hand slips off Tattoo Guy's arm. "Come on, Maxine. Let's go."

Maxine. Ugh. I hate that name. Hate that girl, who thinks she's so much better than me. That she has something I don't . . .

And Gregory . . . I can't believe the things he said to her about me.

As soon as they walk out the door I look at Tattoo Guy again. There's obviously some serious hate going on between the two. Red's claims hit me again. He feels *sorry* for me? Misplaced *obligation*? Screw him! This guy would be the perfect way to get back at Gregory.

A weird, desperate feeling overcomes me. It's so strong that it makes me feel reckless.

I'm not proud to admit this, but after Tattoo Guy gets his coffee and leaves, I throw my purse over my shoulder, grab my caramel macchiato and then I'm out the door behind him. He has long legs and mine are short so I have to jog to catch up. Not that I know what I'm going to say when I get there, but that's beside the point.

"Hey!" Gah. What's his name? "You. Hey, you with the tattoos."

He stops and turns, then waits as I catch up with him. "Hi . . . um . . . hi." I stumble. The first thing I notice is he's pretty, too, but in a totally different way than Gregory. He has great lips, straight teeth. His eyes are incredible. Bright blue, somehow darker toward the center and get lighter on the outside. Definitely pretty, but with an edge to him that Gregory doesn't have.

Pull it together, Chey.

"Hi. I'm Cheyenne." I hold out my hand to him. At first I think he's going to walk away and ignore me, but then he shifts and grabs my hand.

"Colt."

"Colt?"

"Are you really approaching me to talk shit about my name, Princess?" His voice is slightly softer than when he spoke to Gregory, but not much.

"You're right. I just . . ." *Have no idea what to say*. But then I think of how Gregory looked with Maxine. The heated anger that passed between him and Colt. The way I felt when I walked in on Gregory with her.

"So . . . that guy in there?" I say. "The one who was sort of a jerk to you?"

"Frat boy, dickhead? What about him? Friend of yours?" He smirks.

My recklessness fades, leaving the panic that I hate. It pisses me off. I'm not supposed to lose the strength. The new Cheyenne is all strength.

"You know what? Never mind." Turning, I take a few steps away from him.

"Suit yourself," he says behind me. I don't know why, but his response surprises me. Isn't he the least bit curious what I was going to say?

"Do you have a girlfriend?" I blurt. This stops him.

Colt turns and looks at me, one of his eyebrows cocked. "Are you hitting on me, Princess? No thanks. I'm not the kind of guy you can piss off your parents with by slumming."

And just that simple, he starts to walk away. I'm still trying to figure out what just happened. This guy didn't even give me a chance to explain. That's not the part that pisses me off though. I run to catch up. "You don't know me, so don't pretend you do. I don't have parents to piss off. And, I wasn't hitting on you."

I expect him to ask about the parent comment. I'm a little surprised I even said it, but he doesn't. Amusement bounces off his words when he says, "You weren't hitting on me, but you followed me out of the coffee shop and now want to know if I have a girl? I don't know whether to be offended or flattered."

His words and our fast pace make me stumble. He reaches out his hand and catches me. It's warm and calloused and I jerk my arm away. "You don't have to be an asshole about it. Not that I was flirting with you, but still."

"Listen, if there's a point, you need to get to it. I have somewhere I need to be."

It takes a minute for me to reply. I consider walking away, but I can't get Maxine and Gregory out of my head. The way he threw me away. I swore I'd never be thrown away again.

People always fall at Gregory's feet. I loved that about him. This guy? He didn't. That's what I need.

My head high, I tell him, "You never answered the question."

He groans as though he's about done with me, but then he answers. "No, Princess. I don't have a girl. I'm not looking for one either."

The princess thing is about to piss me off, but I let it go. "Good. I'm not either." He grins and I realize what I've said. "I'm not looking for a boyfriend! You know what I mean." Do lesbian jokes ever get old to men?

"Tick tock."

"I have a question for you and it's very private . . . Colt. It wouldn't be good for this to get out."

Which is putting it mildly. Talk about ruining my reputation—my plan. Having it get out that I'm trying to score a fake man would do that more than anything.

He crosses his arms and I try not to study his tattoos. "I'm all ears."

Or all attitude.

"That guy you just got in an argument with?"

His jaw tightens and he nods. Someone walks around us on the sidewalk and I wait until they're gone until I finish. He's going to want all the answers. I know it. A guy like him won't be willing to do this regardless. I'm nauseous at the thought.

"He's my ex-boyfriend. We've been together forever and I just found out he cheated on me. I walked in on it, actually, and I kind of made him think I had another boyfriend to make him jealous. So now I need that. A boyfriend I mean."

Oh. My. God. My stomach drops out. I said it. I really put it out there.

Colt's eyes get huge, and he stares at me for what feels like forever. He opens his mouth and I'm waiting to hear what he'll say, but it's not words that come out. He laughs. Hard. Much harder than he did in the coffee house.

My face is hot. I'm not sure if it's anger or embarrassment or both.

"Very funny, Princess." When he tries to walk away, I grab his arm. His corded muscles tense beneath my hand.

"I'm serious! Do you think I would make something like that up?"

He stops and studies me. I almost want to turn away. No one really looks at me like they're trying to figure me out. They all know who I am now, but this guy, it's like he's looking for something deeper. Something I don't want to be there.

"You really are serious, aren't you? Didn't I just tell you I'm not looking for a girl? I have much more serious shit on my plate than playing this game with you."

"I don't really want to be your girlfriend! It's a charade. Hello? I would figure that much would be obvious." Is he dense, or what?

Colt moves and his arm pulls out of my grasp. "And why would I do this? I don't even know you and I'm definitely not that hard up."

Ugh. Perv. "It's not like I really want you either and I could find someone I like, if I wanted. The point is, I don't."

I'm never giving someone that kind of power over me again. The more I think about it, the more appealing a fake boyfriend is at the moment.

"Forget it," Colt says. "Good luck, Princess."

He's walking away. My one chance to save face is walking away, and I can feel myself clinging, needing something, anything.

"I'll pay you!" I say to his back.

He freezes. Turns. By the way his face hardens and his jaw ticks, I can tell my offer didn't go over very well.

"Wrong answer. I don't need your money."

And with that, he walks away.

CHAPTER FOUR

COLT

I don't do pity. I don't know or honestly give a shit if that chick is serious about what she just asked me, but I can tell you, offering charity isn't going to fly with me. Even though honestly, the money would be nice. It would help.

Regardless, it's not like I would play some stupid game with her anyway. I have too much shit going on to add a spoiled princess to the stack.

Even if she is hot as hell.

I've always been into girls with dark hair. Her skin is a smooth, even shade of brown with legs that are short, but firm. I can definitely picture them wrapped around my waist.

Luckily for me, she spoke and ruined it.

Pity isn't the only thing I don't do. Princesses are high on my list too.

Though if she was on the real, it would feel good to stick it to Pretty Boy.

Again.

I hate assholes like him who think they own the

fucking world and can get away with whatever they want. He's a bully and I hate people who throw their weight around like that. So I showed him how it felt to be picked on.

I walk across the street tossing a look over my shoulder. Princess is walking away, her hips swaying back and forth as she goes. She knows how hot she is.

Nope. This girl isn't someone I want to screw around with.

My cell beeps. It's Adrian so I pick it up, knowing he probably has something going on that I need. "Hey."

"Hey, man. What's up?"

"Nothing. Just leaving school and heading home."

"You got anything?"

My gut tightens after he asks. Yeah, I've always known I wouldn't amount to shit, but I never saw this for myself. It would kill Mom. "Depends on how much you need." I only deal in weed so there's no point in asking what he wants.

"An eighth. It's for a friend who stopped by."

"We're good. I'll be there in a few," I tell him.

I hang up wondering if this was how stuff started for my dad. If he did it just to help out, but things got out of control. Nah. Not him. I hate that prick. He was always letting Mom down. I can't be like that.

Can't.

CHAPTER FIVE

CHEYENNE

The next day, I still can't get over Tattoo Guy. I mean, what was his problem? I didn't do anything to him. Even if he didn't want to go through with it, he didn't have to be such a jerk about it.

It's always the hot ones who are assholes. I used to think Gregory was the exception. Obviously I was wrong there.

My heart is beating about a million miles an hour as I get ready to go to class. With Gregory. And if I remember correctly, Red, who I never paid much attention to, but will now.

I'd rather my heart didn't beat at all if that didn't mean I was—well, dead. But I can feel my control slipping. Feel myself getting panicky. Again. That's what I hate Gregory for the most. I finally have the control I need and he's taken that away from me. He makes me feel like I'm going to have a breakdown. That's not something I'll let myself do. I won't lose it.

When I lift my brush to my hair, my hands are shaking. Shaking. Get it together, Chey. I concentrate on running the brush through my chocolate-brown hair. It reminds me of Hershey Bars—which brings a memory of Mom flooding back to the surface. She loved chocolate. I remember a time when we had it for dinner for three days straight.

Fighting back those thoughts, I brush again, letting it take the tremor out of my hands. That's one memory I don't mind letting drift to the surface—for a few seconds at least. Mom always used to brush my hair and I loved it. It made me feel taken care of when I was anything but.

My dorm room door opens and Andy walks in. She scans me quickly before saying, "You look nice. Don't tell me you're dressing up for your ex." She walks past me and flops onto her bed.

"Umm, thanks?" I'm not sure what else to say.

"Holy shit. Don't tell me you're going to be like that. Don't get all stressed out because I told you I like girls and then said you look nice."

"What?" I whip around. I hadn't even thought of that. "I didn't even think about that, thank you very much. I just don't get why you think I'm dressing up." I look down at my mini-skirt and wedges. The skirt is purple and my tank top's white. I'm not sure what's so dressed up about it.

"You dress like that every day?"

"Why wouldn't I?" I love my clothes. Love that I have them. I didn't always.

Andy shrugs, but I can see her looking down at me. Her nose is crinkled and I bet she doesn't know it. I want to tell her she doesn't know what it's like—to go from having nothing to having everything. To wearing the same thing for days and then having so many clothes to choose from that I lost count. "There's nothing wrong with wanting to look good."

She shakes her pink-haired head at me as though she thinks I'm ridiculous. I'm about to tell her where she can stick it when she says, "There's a party tonight. It's supposed to be a good one. You're welcome to come with Veronica and me."

"Oh . . . um . . ." The truth is, I'm not sure I can go to a party without Gregory. I'm always a little nervous at them. I got over it, because that's what I do, but I'm also close to having panic attacks again too.

Gregory doesn't even know I have them it's been so long, yet now I can't seem to stop my fingers from curling and my chest from feeling tight.

That's not all.

I hate admitting it, even to myself, but what if he's there with her? Will I be able to handle it? And . . . I don't really know Andy either. What if we don't get along? What if they leave me? I don't want to be alone. Can't.

"Just an offer. You don't have to hyperventilate."

I turn away from her, busying myself with makeup. I am breathing heavy. I can't believe I'm getting so worked up over this.

"I'll help you find your mama."

Just like they did all those years ago, my eyes start to sting. Liquid drips over the brim, but this time it's colored with my makeup.

"Hey, are you okay?"

I concentrate on my words as I speak them. "Yeah. Fine. I just poked my eye."

I do everything to try and fight this off. I'm over it. Past it. The new Cheyenne who doesn't have such a screwed up past.

"I can't do the party tonight. I forgot I have plans."

I hate Gregory even more for unearthing my past. Maybe it's me I should hate for letting it slip back in, just because of a guy.

Or maybe it was never gone in the first place.

I walk into class right before it starts. My head is high, no sign of the tears that tried to drown me earlier. I'm over it now. Gregory, Maxine or anyone else isn't worth becoming that scared, lonely girl I was when Mom would leave me. I won't let myself be the one left behind again.

I don't keep my eyes from scanning the room. Not in a needy way, but in a nonchalant, I-don't-give-a-shit one. I catch Gregory's eye across the room and don't turn away. He gives me a small smile, which I don't return, before he looks away. I sit tall, hands shaking in my lap proud I'm not coming apart. All sewn up tight the way I'm supposed to be.

I take my time gathering my things when class is over. Not because I'm weak and can't handle seeing Gregory and Red. Whatever. I'm over them, but I'm tired from lack of sleep and I'm not going to be that girl who has to rush out of class so I don't run into them.

I hear her laugh and I cringe, accidentally knocking my stuff to the floor. Great.

By the time I make it out, the large room is empty except for my professor who's not paying me any attention. I leave the room and step into the busy hall. People carry books, coffees, weaving around me like I'm not there. My stomach suddenly aches.

I turn, ready to head to my next class when I see them. Gregory and Red. He has her pressed against the wall, his lips on hers and his hips grinding into her. Yes. Right there for the world to see. I want to puke. The jerk has been calling me non-stop, leaving voicemails and he's making out with her right in front of me?

Who the hell is this guy?

"Don't cry, Princess. You know what they say. You

have to kiss a lot of frogs before you meet your prince."

I recognize the voice of Tattoo Guy right away. I turn around to tell him where he can stick it, but he's already walking away from me.

Screw him.

Screw Gregory.

And screw anyone else who tries to shove me aside. I'm fine on my own. I'm going to that party tonight and I'm going to prove them all wrong.

CHAPTER SIX

COLT

When Adrian said the frat guys were having a party, I was definitely down. Crashing pretty boy parties is always a good time. Plus, it's a good chance for me to make money. Frat boys are some of my best customers. Let's not forget I also get to meet girls—both things that are high on my list.

Before I head out I stop by Mom's house. She sounded like shit when I talked to her on the phone today. I get a knot in my gut every time I think about seeing her and then I feel like a pussy because I'm her son and she's dying. I should be able to handle it better than that. For her.

For some reason, my heart jackhammers when I step inside the apartment. I run a hand through my hair, which annoys the shit out of me. I hate nervous habits like that.

"She's sleeping, Colton," Maggie says from the kitchen.

I make a turn and head toward her. "How's she doing? How'd her appointment go today?"

Maggie sighs. Her gray hair is tied back in a bun that disappears when she turns to face me. "They've added another medication. It's stronger to help with the nausea and vomiting. Also more pain meds."

I lean against the table. "Fuck."

"Do you kiss your mama with that mouth?"

I know she's trying to make me smile, but I can't right now. "Not in the mood, Maggie."

She walks over to me, a sad look in her dark eyes. I know this is almost as hard on her as it is me. She's the best friend Mom's ever had.

"How much, Maggie?"

"You don't want to know, Colton."

"And the lease is up in two weeks. You know they always raise the rent when it's time to sign a new lease. Hospice will take care of the meds, I'm more worried about rent and bills."

Will she need a new lease? As soon as the thought crosses my mind, I feel like the world's biggest prick. She will. She has to.

"Fuck," I ground out again. Does it ever stop? Jesus, she's done nothing but try her whole life. She's been there for me, worked her ass off and when she could have easily left me behind like Dad did. She didn't. Not when Dad was in and out of jail. Not when we ate Top Ramen every day.

This is the payment she gets?

"I'll pick up some more hours. Maybe do some odd jobs or something." Maggie touches my hand and I say, "I should have gone. I was wasting my time in a stupid classroom today and I should have been with her."

"You know she wants you in the classroom. You're going to live her dreams and that's what matters to her."

I don't reply to that, but say, "I'm gonna go in and see her."

I make my way to Mom's room. She's lying in bed so still, looking ghost white. My heart drops somewhere to my feet. Holy shit, she looks dead. She can't fucking be dead, can she?

"Didn't anyone ever tell you it's rude to stare?" Mom's eyes flutter open. I let out a heavy breath.

"My mom tried to teach me manners, but they didn't stick so well," I tease as I walk into the room.

"Yes they did. You just like to pretend they didn't."

I pull up a chair beside her bed. It's so different when they know you're dying and they can't do anything about it. No hospitals. All there is to do is wait. And medicate. Always medicate.

"How you feeling?" I'm not in the mood to pretend to be happy.

"Happy to see my son. What are you doing tonight? Have big plans with your friends?" There's a small smile on her lips, but they're dry. Too dry.

I pick up the cup from beside her bed. "Let me help

you get a drink." I put the straw by her mouth, but she shakes her head and a shaky hand grabs the glass.

"I can do it, Colton. I don't like you having to take care of me."

Someone should. She deserves it. It's not like she hasn't done it for others.

"I thought I'd hang with you tonight. Maybe watch a movie or something."

Mom takes a small sip and I grab the cup from her, putting it back on the bedside table. "You're not staying with me tonight. You go have fun. I'll still be here tomorrow."

Maybe.

"There's nothing going on," I lie.

"Liar," she tosses back at me and her attitude does make me smile. "You're covered in too much ink." She slides her fragile finger down my arm. "You're too handsome to be so covered up." I open my mouth to reply, but she cuts me off. "Go out tonight. I'll be fine. I want you to have fun. If you try to stay, I'll make Maggie kick you out."

I know her well enough to know she's not screwing around. "Mom . . ."

"Colton . . ."

I shake my head at her. "I love you. Get some rest, alright?" I push to my feet. Mom smiles and it makes that knot it my gut multiply. Still, I listen to her and go.

*   *   *

Two kegs are in the living room—both with lines behind them, but in one line, everyone has cups and in the other, they're doing keg stands. Adrian's bouncing on his heels beside me, his dark hair hanging in his eyes.

"I'm ready to get my party on. Find me a rich girl or two to have my way with."

I try to laugh at him. "Multiples now?"

"There's a first time for everything." Adrian holds out his fist and I hit it.

"I need a drink." We head through the room. I have a flask in my pocket, but I'd rather drink their shit than mine. The kitchen is our first stop. The fridge is packed with anything we could want to drink.

Bottles in hand, we go back toward the living room. My eyes scan the room looking for, hell, I don't even know what. That's when I see Princess walk in with two other chicks. The girls are holding hands and you can tell Princess is trying to keep some space from them. She obviously doesn't want it known she's here with them, but then I can't help but wonder why she is.

Dollar signs pop into my head as she walks through the room, her head high with those slender legs. Her skirt is short. Her dark hair long and straight, but somehow looking like she spent hours on it. I think she's Indian or something. Whatever the fuck she is, she's gorgeous. And she offered me money that would probably help pay for my mom's shit. Rent. Everything else.

Hell no. What am I thinking? I couldn't go through with that. She'd drive me up the fucking wall.

"What ya looking at, man?" Adrian asks. I nod my head toward Princess. "Day-um."

"No shit. She's a spoiled brat though. She was doin' that frat boy we got into it with."

"Greg or whatever the hell his name is?"

"Yep."

Which is another reason I can't deal with her. I have too much on my plate to deal with a spoiled princess and her douchebag ex.

"I fucking hate that guy," Adrian yells.

Him and me both.

Princess walks away and I forget about her. The bottle is in my hand, but I haven't taken one drink. I don't know what the hell is wrong with me, but I'm just not feeling it.

It isn't long before Adrian's off with some chick. I'm wondering if I should do the same thing just to get my mind off stuff, every time someone comes up to me, I keep shooting them down.

I wander the place for an hour talking to people before I'm sick of the whole thing. I head outside when I see Princess without her two friends, but with the asshole Greg. My hands squeeze into a fist. Jesus, it would feel good to hit him. Hit something, anything, to see if it took any of the pain away. Instead I duck around the corner and wonder what the hell has gotten into me.

"Come on, babe. You know I love you. I was just screwing around with Maxine. You're the one I want."

"Then you shouldn't have screwed around. You messed up, Gregory and I moved on."

Ah, so she must have found her fake boyfriend. Or she has a real one. I can't believe she wants to make this prick jealous so bad that she'd go there.

"I'm sorry. Damn you look sexy tonight."

Again my hands fist. Even if I didn't hate the guy, he'd deserve the shit knocked out of him right now.

"Too bad for you. You can look, but you can't touch anymore."

I'm surprised the princess has it in her. Most girls would fall down to whatever he says, but she's standing her own.

"Cheyenne. Don't be like this."

"I—" she starts, but then she's cut off and there's a muffled sound.

I look around the corner again and he's kissing her. Looks like she didn't hold her ground for long. I'm about to walk away, when I see she's trying to push him off her. Fucking prick. It's going to feel good to hit this guy.

I head for them. I don't get very far before she's

ripping herself away from him and a group of people walk around the corner closest to them.

"Gregory, what are you doing?" Some red-headed chick says. She's surrounded by more of the frat guys.

"Just having a talk with Cheyenne. We had a few things to work out."

The red head smiles. "I see you left your girlfriends behind. Is that who you were talking about? Playing for the other team now?"

Rolling your eyes is such a bullshit thing to do, but I do it anyway. Is that the best she can come up with?

"No, actually, I was trying to keep your boyfriend from kissing me."

I can't help it. I laugh. Princess has balls.

"What the fuck, Cheyenne!" Gregory says. His friends are all laughing. Red-head is scowling. And I can see the tenseness in Princess's body.

"You know that's not how it happened," Greg adds. "Maxine, I didn't try to kiss her, it was the other way around. I called her on the fake boyfriend and she kissed me."

Then, I'm walking forward. I don't know what in the fuck I'm doing, but I can't stop myself. This guy is a prick. I need the money and I'd like nothing more than to kill two birds with one stone by scoring some cash and sticking it to him.

"Hey, you. There you are." I step up beside Princess

and wrap my arm around her waist. She tenses more, before looking over at me. There's fire in her dark brown eyes, but she manages a smile.

"I was looking for you . . ."

Shit. She forgot my name. Leaning forward, I kiss the side of her mouth before she can reply. "You found me. Or I found you. Whatever it is, I'm here. Are these pricks bothering you?" I pull her to me and now the fire is directed at me. She's pissed, but if I'm going there, I'm making this shit look real.

"Him? You're dating this guy? He's a loser, Chey."

With that I step away from the princess and head straight for Greg. "You don't want to piss me off tonight—actually, you do. I'm begging you to fucking piss me off, man. Give me an excuse to kick your ass again."

The look on his face makes this whole charade worth it.

CHAPTER SEVEN

CHEYENNE

Kick his ass again? Okay, so obviously Colt and Gregory have gotten into it, which as the ex-girlfriend of two years, I should probably know. He never even told me he'd gotten into a fight. Though I guess in the grand scheme of things that went on behind my back, this one is minor compared to the other.

Still . . . I hate fighting. Hate it, so I step between them, willing my anxiety to stay locked away. I stumble a little, the alcohol starting to affect me. "Okay, that's enough of the testosterone fest, boys." I look at Gregory. "Yes, I'm with him, though I'm not sure that's your business." For added effect I grab onto Colt's arm. Or maybe it's because I'm suddenly feeling a little woozy.

And, damn, are his arms firm. Does this boy live in a gym or something?

"G—honey, maybe we should go." Red has her cocky smile. The one that says she thinks I'm out here pining for her boyfriend. That he's being a gentleman by worrying about his poor, little ex-girlfriend.

Gregory's face is pale. Jaw stiff. He definitely doesn't like the idea of me being with Colt.

Colt doesn't touch me back. It feels as though someone injected cement into him as tense as he is. The only thing moving is his chest, up and down from heavy breathing. Wow. He's taking this much more seriously than I thought he would. Or he hates Gregory more than I thought he did.

"Gregory . . . let's go. They're not worth it." Red pulls him back as Colt steps forward.

"Are we not worth it or are you too scared?"

Gregory gives his cocky grin and I start to feel a little nervous. Gregory has a friend with him and Colt doesn't. I have no doubt who would win one on one, but the odds aren't in Colt's favor.

"What do we have here? Why didn't you tell me we moved the party outside, Colt?" A guy steps up beside us. He's got nearly as many tattoos as Colt does, but he has dark hair. Short and spikey, and he's tall. Taller than Colt or Gregory.

"Party hasn't started yet," Colt replies simply.

I'm willing to admit this might be getting out of hand. Starting a brawl is not something I'm into. All I want to do is show Gregory I don't need him. That I'm better off without him.

"Gregory . . . take me home. I can think of

something much better we can do," Red says. Yep, I'm going to puke. Definitely going to vomit.

Gregory eyes Colt and then his friend before shaking his head. "You can have her. She's not worth all the trouble. I'm not the first one to think so either." He backs up before looping his arm through Red's. He used to do that with me. Dizziness hits me again, but I try to fight it down. *I'm not the first one to think so either . . .*

He might not have known everything about me, but he knew Mom left me. He was supposed to be safe, but he's throwing that back at me.

Relax, relax, relax.

When Gregory, Red and his friend walk around the corner, Colt jerks away from me, almost making me lose my balance. Somehow I keep the panic at bay, but he's obviously not doing as well.

"Fuck!" Colt yells. His face is red and I'm pretty sure he might explode at any second.

"Simmer down," I tell him though I feel like doing the same thing. At least I don't show it like he does.

"Hey, baby. I don't think we've met. I'm Adrian," his friend steps up to me.

I roll my eyes, but Colt answers before I can. "Back off, Adrian."

"Sorry, man. Didn't know she was your girl."

I open my mouth to say I'm not, but then remember I am. Well, that I'm supposed to be. I think.

"Sexist, much?" is what I decide on.

Adrian grins and Colt steps up to us again. "Not now." He shakes his head and his blond hair falls in front of his eyes. Colt pushes it back and talks to his friend. "I gotta get the hell out of here. You cool? You leaving? I need to have a talk with the princess."

He's going to drive me up the freaking wall. I turn to him. "Stop calling me that!" When I try to take a step, my heel catches on the sidewalk and I fly forward. Colt catches me, that stupid tattooed arm holding me tight. I jerk away.

"Fine," he says. "The drunk princess and I need to have a talk."

Adrian starts to laugh and I'm getting seriously pissed off here. "It's rude to laugh at people." To Colt. "Are you always an asshole?"

"No. There's just something about you that brings it out in me."

I cock my brow at him.

"You're right. I lied. I'm always an asshole."

Adrian jumps in. "I hate to break up the foreplay you guys have going on, but I'm out. I'd much rather party at my own house with my own shit. You coming home?" He looks at me. "Alone? Deena texted, but if you want I'll tell her you're spoken for now."

I can tell Adrian's giving Colt a hard time, and Colt isn't happy about it. Still . . . "Who's Deena? You said you didn't have a girlfriend!"

Colt rolls his eyes.

That's it. I'm over this. I don't need him. I can find someone else. I head toward the front of the house. Colt is right behind me, but I'm trying to ignore him when I realize. "Shit. I don't have my car. I need to find my . . ." I'm not really sure I can call Andy my friend yet.

"Come with me. I'm driving you back."

"I'm pretty sure you just ordered me to do something. You'll get a whole lot further if you ask."

Colt shakes his head. He's got a dimple I notice. It makes him look young . . . sweet. Too bad I know the truth. But he is a contradiction, this guy—all tattoos, clothes that says he doesn't give a shit and bad mouth with the boy-next-door face.

"If you want a ride, you need to come with me. If you want to talk about this stupid game you want to play with your ex, you need to come with me. If you don't, I'm gone. It's been a bad day, Princess."

Bad day. Yeah, I can understand that. Not like I plan on sharing that with him though. Another wave of dizziness hits me. "Fine, I'll go, but it's because I need a ride back to my dorm. Not that I want to go anywhere with you."

"Huh. That's funny. Seems to me you want in my pants—" I cut him a dirty look, but he continues, "Or at least you want people to think you do."

"No, I want them to think I'm already there.

Actually, I want them to think you're in mine, because there's nowhere else you'd rather be. Don't think you'll actually get a peek at the goods, because it's not happening. Now . . . which way to your car?"

I'm all talk. Inside I'm shrinking, hearing Gregory's words, but if anyone knows how to play the game, it's me.

It's never a good idea to drink on an empty stomach. Add in the excitement of a near fight with your ex, only to have your fake boyfriend save the day, and then the quite bumpy ride in his car and your stomach will be done for.

Nausea spreads throughout me. Colt's silent beside me. It's so crazy. I've never gotten why girls go for those closed off, angry, bad boys. Not that I'm going for him, but I've tied myself to him and he's not my kind of guy. I've seen what happens when women let men like Colt into their lives and it doesn't end well. Good thing I hate him.

Colt hits a hole in the road, head on. I swear it makes something shoot up my stomach and almost come out of my mouth. "Are you doing that on purpose?"

"No," is all he says.

I'd already given him directions to my dorm, so he pulls up out front and parks. "How's this going to work, Princess?"

"I can tell you right now it's not going to work if you don't stop calling me that. My name is Cheyenne. Use it. Gregory would know I'd hate a name like that." He ruined my shot at the fairytale. At pretending the girl who lived with Mom wasn't me.

Colt groans. "Let's just get this figured out. I need to know what you expect and how much I'm going to get for it."

I offer him a few hundred dollars, which he agrees to. I'm surprised he didn't ask for more. We decide how often he needs to be seen with me and the kind of things I expect him to do (public displays of affection only, and some flowers and stuff).

"We don't want this relationship to go on too long, because I'll probably go crazy. I'm thinking three weeks and I get to dump you." I smirk at him.

"You care what people think too much. I couldn't give a shit who dumps who, and two weeks, tops."

"Fine," I grit out. I'm starting to wonder if this is going to be worth it. "And it's not that I care what people think it's that . . ."

"That what? Can't handle having a smudge on your reputation? Used to be on top of the world in high school and now you realize none of that matters? Can't handle not having a perfect life? Think you're too good—"

His words are suddenly too much. I don't know if it's how upside down my life feels, the alcohol or what, but I can't keep my mouth shut. "You don't know anything about me so stop pretending you do! I'm not perfect and I never have been! I was the typical little girl with the absentee mom who would rather party than take care of me. Then she dropped me off at my aunt and uncle's one day and never came back. Think what you want about me, but know right now that everything hasn't been perfect for me. It's all a big lie!"

My chest starts to tighten. It's hard to breathe. My head pounds and the dizziness hits again except it's more than drunk-spins. My fingers do their fisting thing that I can't stop. Holy shit. I can't have a panic attack in front of him. Can't be that weak. Not after what I just verbally vomited at him. Why did I say that?

I push out of the car and slam the door behind me. I hear another door slam, but it's almost like an echo. Please don't let him follow me. Please don't let anyone else come out.

Why can't I get it together?

"Cheyenne," he calls after me, but I keep walking. I'm heading toward the street, no clue where I'm going, but I have to get out of here before I lose it.

"Cheyenne. Slow down."

"Leave me alone," I manage to say, but keep going. I won't let him see me like this.

"Fine, I'll say this while we're walking then . . . So what? So what if your mom left you?"

This makes me freeze in my tracks. Suddenly, I don't care if I can breathe anymore. I whip around to face him. "So what? You really are a prick!" I put my hands against his chest and shove. Hard. "I changed my mind. I'm not doing this with you."

I hear him mumble a "fuck", but I don't care. I'm done playing this game with him. I get two steps away when he speaks again. "My mom's dying. I see it every fucking day. I watch her wither away more and more knowing pretty soon she'll be gone."

I want to move . . . to keep walking away, but I can't. It's like he's stripped. All the anger and cockiness is gone from his voice replaced by pain.

I can't make myself turn around to face him, but I still say, "And you deal with it by being an asshole. I deal my way. One isn't better than the other."

"Is that what you're doing? Dealing with it by trying to prove that no one can leave you? That you'll always move on and that you're better than them?"

Part of me wants to shut down. To deny what he says because that quickly, he sees me for exactly who I am. I don't know how to feel about that.

Finally I make myself turn around. We're close to the street, at the far end of the parking lot. There's a light above us, but the night is black. It's like all the alcohol has left my system. The anxiety too. I don't have it in me to feel much right now. "Just like you try and show no emotions. You don't feel anything. Like you hate the world."

It's strange, having this conversation about appearances with him. This guy I don't know . . . and don't really like, yet I'm letting him see me naked—those dark hidden places inside me that I've never shown before. "Are you going to tell anyone?" I try to look him in the eyes.

"No. Your business. Not mine." Colt sighs. "I'm not easy to get along with. You're asking for a long ass two weeks, Princess."

"I'm not easy to get along with either and I told you I'm not your princess."

"I need the money."

"I need . . . this." Need to save face. Need to show I can move forward.

He shakes his head and rubs his left hand up and down his opposite arm. The tattooed one.

Then, he does the strangest thing. Colt grins. I'm sure it's fake and it's probably the one he uses to get girls into bed, but it's so out of place here that I can't help but study it.

"Then come on, sweetheart. What kind of boyfriend would I be if I didn't make sure my girl got to her room okay?"

CHAPTER EIGHT

COLT

I feel like such a prick, which isn't usually something I let myself worry about. There's way more important things to think about than hurting someone's delicate sensibilities, but when this girl admitted what she did about her mom—and I reacted like I always do—I felt like shit.

Still feel like shit.

But I still can't believe I'm doing this. It pisses me off I have to do this. That after Mom's spent her life trying to take care of everyone, she has to die and still worry about how she'll pay the rent.

And here I am practically selling myself by calling a truce with this girl and pretending to be her guy. I let out a small laugh.

"What?" she asks.

"I was just thinking this is one fucked up game of charades we're playing."

She ignores that, but says, "Who's Deena? I can't do this if you're with someone."

"I'm not. In case you didn't notice, I'm not really

the boyfriend type. We've hooked up. We hook up when we want to, but neither of us wants anything serious. There are no attachments."

"Is she going to be a problem?"

I shake my head even though she's not looking at me. "No, but I'll tell her what's up—"

"No! You can't tell anyone—"

"That I'm selling myself to you?"

"Ugh. You're not. It's not real. It's not like anything is really going to happen between us." She says it with a sneer.

"Believe me. I don't want you either. You're too damn high maintenance."

"I am not!"

"And I'm not going there with you. I'm tired, pissed off and done fighting. Let's just get you inside so I can go." It's going to be a long ass two weeks.

"Fine. Whatever."

We get up to her building and I open the door for her. She cocks her head at me, but then shakes it off. "What? Think I'm a fucking Neanderthal who doesn't know how to treat a girl?"

"No. Neanderthals have better mouths than you do."

A laugh jumps out of my mouth, surprising me. I can't even remember the last time I laughed and it puts me on edge. I suddenly want to do the same thing to her. Let her see how it feels to teeter on that cliff.

I turn and face her, taking steps toward Cheyenne instead of the door. She backs up and I move forward. When she hits the wall, I keep going. Each of my hands are on the wall, one on each side of her head. She sucks in a quick breath and I falter a little, before catching myself. Closer . . . I lean closer until my lips are right next to her ear. She smells a little like alcohol, but also like some kind of perfume too.

"I think you'd like my mouth, Princess. I've never had any complaints. I promise, it'll make you feel good."

She gasps and I suddenly want to make good on my threat. I want to suck the lobe of her ear into my mouth. Kiss the spot behind it to see if it drives her wild.

"Colt . . ."

"Yeah," I inhale. Damn, she's kind of sexy. I feel her body against mine and I want more.

"If you don't step away from me right now, your mouth will be the only thing left you have to make girls feel good with."

Her words snap me out of whatever trance I was in. No, I'm not going to go there with this girl, but I am going to have fun with her. "Why? Are you scared you won't be able to keep your hands off me? Might want this to be a little more than a game?"

I feel her breath against my face. My dick reacts to how close she is, but I'm still not moving away.

"Does this usually work on girls?" Her voice is raspier than it was earlier.

"It's working now."

She makes almost a squealing noise and I know I've got her. She wants me—Cheyenne pushes me out of the way, catching me off guard. Turning she pukes all over the floor.

"Fuck." I run a hand through my hair. How the hell is it a girl can seem fine one minute and she's puking the next. "Can you walk?"

Cheyenne looks at me from her bent over position, rolls her eyes and says, "Of course I can walk." She stands and straightens her clothes. I have to give it to her for trying, but she makes it two steps before she's grabbing the wall.

I should walk out. I don't have time for this and more importantly I don't want to deal with it, but instead I step up to her. "Put your arms around my neck and don't argue or I'm gone."

She does as I say and I lift her in my arms. We walk inside and don't make it very far before a girl shrieks.

"You're going to get in trouble for being here. You're lucky they're not at the desk."

Sure enough there's a big ass desk sitting there. Fuck. I forgot about all the dorm rules.

"There's no way I can help her upstairs? She likes me to help her get undressed," I tease.

"Asshole," Princess mumbles.

The other girl giggles.

"There's nothing I can do?"

"I'm okay, I can make it," Princess says.

The girl standing there jumps in, "I'll help her," but she's looking at me the whole time.

I nod at her and wink. Seeing a pad of paper on the desk I grab a piece and a pen.

I start to write her name, but scratch it out. If I'm going to play this game, I'm going to do it right.

Babe,

Call me.

Colt.

I leave my number below my name. I shove the paper in her hand. I stand there watching while the girl helps Cheyenne down the hall. I watch till they're gone.

What the fuck have I gotten myself into?

The house is packed when I get home. I think about partying, but I'm beat. I find Deena, peel her off me and tell her I'm with someone now. She laughs because she knows I don't do the dating thing, but I leave it at that. I did my part.

I'm in bed about an hour when my cell rings. I don't know the number, but I pick it up anyway. "Yeah?"

"Hey . . ."

It's Cheyenne.

"Is getting phone calls all through the night part of this gig?"

She sounds half asleep and again I feel like a dick for being an ass.

"Thanks . . . I just wanted to say thanks. For everything. And for making sure someone helped me get inside."

Her words shock the hell out of me. Does this pseudo-princess really feel like she's always going to get ditched? That she has to cling to this image to make herself worth something? It's screwed up.

But I don't care, either. I don't even like the girl. I have this stupid, fucking promise I made bearing down on me and a mom who's dying. That's what's important.

"It's gonna cost you extra."

I don't even know if she heard me because the line is dead.

CHAPTER NINE

CHEYENNE

I feel like shit. It's crazy how you can drink and think you're okay until you're suddenly not okay. When Colt got close, I suddenly wasn't okay anymore.

All those sinewy muscles up close and personal and tribal tattoos right there for me to dissect. The roughness of his voice. In all the times I got hot and heavy with Gregory he never sounded like that and with Colt, we weren't even doing anything. I remember Mom telling me there's something in a man's voice . . . in the inflection or how he talks to you or about you that says a lot. I never thought about it until now and I can't help but wonder what Colt's voice meant.

Besides the fact that he was turned on. Yeah, I felt that too, right before I lost it.

I get out of bed and brush my teeth. No point lying around all day going over something that doesn't matter.

Because it doesn't.

Matter, I mean.

Just to prove it I pick up my phone and call him using the number on the paper he gave me. I have no idea how early his classes are, but mine start soon and if he's going to do this, I need him to do it all the way.

"What?" His voice is even gruffer than it was last night.

"That's no way to talk to the love of your life."

"I'm not a morning person, Prin—Cheyenne. Spit it out before I hang up on you the way you did to me last night."

Hang up on him? Oh shit. I did call him last night. I can't believe I forgot that. Why did I do that?

"Tick tock," he says like he did the first day we met. I'm about to call him on being an asshole again, but I don't have the time right now.

"What time are your classes? I need you to meet me at 10:40. Gregory and Red are in that class so it would be nice if you picked me up."

"Would it?" He sounds out of breath.

"What are you doing? Why do you sound like that?"

There's a pause on the other side of the line before he says . . . "Did you ever think you caught me in the middle of something? You know how guys are in the morning, and I did get left high and dry last—"

"Colt! Oh my God. You're disgusting. I swear you're

the crudest person I ever met." I'm trying to yell over his laugher. It's the first time I've heard him really let go.

"You asked." He says no apologies. I'm sure he's lying. Pretty sure. He has to be, right?

"I hate you."

"Right back at ya. So where do you need me to parade around and show you off? I have other stuff to do today."

I tell him which class I'm in and he agrees to meet me.

Long after we hang up, I still have his rough voice in my mind. Even a few pictures of him doing exactly what he said he was doing. Which makes for a nice image, but one I need to find a way to kick out of my mind.

After running down the hall to shower, I get dressed in a skirt, tank, and another shirt over it that hangs off my shoulder. I leave my hair down, throw on a pair of wedges to give me height and head to class.

No, it's not the best outfit to wear to school, but it works.

The second I walk into the large, oval shaped room, I see Gregory. He stares me down, his eyes narrowed. I give him my best smile. Gregory takes a step toward me when the professor walks in and starts talking.

I feel his eyes on my back the whole class. Take that, Gregory. This is what you get for throwing me away.

"I'm not the first one to think so either." I try to block out his words.

As soon as class ends, I head toward the door.

"Chey! Wait up!" Gregory shouts from behind me, but I keep going. Colt better be outside this door right now.

Better. Be.

"I don't have time, Gregory," I say over my shoulder. Stepping into the busy hallway, I look around. Of course. Colt isn't here.

"Chey." He grabs my wrist. "I just want to talk."

Red has her arms crossed, but she's standing a few feet away from us. Part of me wants to gloat, but I'm too annoyed.

"I'm pretty sure you don't have the right to grab me." I've been grabbed against my will before and I'm not about to let it happen again. I jerk my hand away.

"Sorry, sorry. You're right. I'm worried about you, Cheyenne. That guy? He's unstable. He seriously attacked us when we were out one night. You're not being yourself and I want to make sure everything's okay."

His voice is sugary sweet. It's the voice he uses to get his way. I've heard it a million times, except he used to use it on other people and not me.

It reminds me of what this is all about. Gregory's used to having his way. Winning. He never expected me to walk away. He wanted to have his cake and eat it too. Or to screw around with Red, but have me on his arm. Not going to happen.

So I play the game too. "I'm better than okay, actually. Colt . . . he . . ." I use the same fakeness on him, as though I'm so enamored with Colt that I can't find the words to explain him when really I want to use a few choice words that wouldn't help my situation.

"You're going to get hurt. He's using you to get in your pants."

Now this pissed me off. "Excuse me? You're the one who—"

"This is the second time I've caught you messing with my girl, Pretty Boy. I'm not going to let it go a third time."

I can't believe it, but I actually exhale a sigh of relief at the sound of Colt's voice. Colt pulls me in front of him, and puts his hands on my waist. Under my shirt. They're warm against my skin. "Hey. Sorry I'm late." He leans forward and presses his lips to my neck and holy shit, I shiver. He's good at this.

"H—hey." Ugh. Why is my voice breaking? I need to get myself together.

"You're done here, right? I really want to get you alone." He kisses my neck again. Even nibbles on it a little and out of nowhere I giggle. Okay. I need to chill and I don't remember telling him he could kiss me, but there's no way I'm stopping him now.

Gregory is just watching us, eyes wide. Fire burns in them and I know he wants to explode, but I also know he's probably afraid of Colt. This couldn't be more perfect.

"Yeah. I'm definitely ready."

"Catch ya later, Pretty Boy." I hear the grin in Colt's voice. He latches our hands together, and we walk away, while I try to ignore the tingles shooting around in my stomach.

CHAPTER TEN

COLT

The second we step outside, I let go of her hand. I'm not a real hand-holding-kind-of-guy, especially when I'm not really hooking up with the girl. The kissing? That I can handle, but the rest of it is too frolicking-through-flowers for my taste.

"What was that?" Cheyenne asks, her mouth pursed.

"That was me making the asshole jealous, like you're paying me to."

"You didn't have to really kiss me."

I look at her. Would it hurt to show a little appreciation? "You're just pissed you liked it."

"We should go to the coffee house. It'll be good for us to make an appearance together."

"Choosing to ignore what I just said to you? And what if I have a class? Or do you?"

She shakes her head. "I have a little break before my next one. You?"

For the first time since coming outside she looks

at me. Christ, she's gorgeous. This would be a whole hell of a lot easier if she wasn't. She has these pouty, little lips I want to bite and then suck into my mouth.

"Are you checking me out?"

Fuck. I got caught. "Do you have to ask? You know how you look."

This makes her stumble. I try to catch her, but she does it herself. "I . . ."

I shake my head. "I don't play games, Cheyenne. I tell it how it is. The only games here are the ones you're paying me to play around everyone else."

"Can we just go get a coffee now?" She's fighting a smile which honestly, makes her sexier. Too bad she drives me crazy.

"Anything you want, Princess Cheyenne." I don't know why it is, but I can't stop screwing with this girl. She both pisses me off and makes me feel mischievous at the same time.

"I thought you were going to stop calling me that?"

"I thought you were going to stop acting like a princess?"

She sighs and for the first time I wonder if this whole thing is wearing on her more than I thought. "Why don't our truces last very long?" she asks.

"I guess we're special like that." Again, I feel like an ass. I don't know why I'm worried about it. We'll be going our separate ways in no time.

"Let's just go get coffee so you can show me off," she says.

We walk to the coffee house I first saw her at. When we get inside I ask her what she wants and tell her she can sit while I order. Such a good little lap dog I'm becoming.

Cheyenne smiles at me. A few minutes later I'm at the table with our drinks and sit down.

"So . . ." she's obviously reaching for something to say. Instead of saving her, I sit back to see what she'll come up with. "Classes. You never replied about classes."

"I'm good till later today."

"How old are you?"

"Shouldn't you already know this, since we're sleeping together?" I wink at her.

"You know what? Never mind. I forgot how big an asshole you are."

I sigh. What is it with this woman? "Twenty-one. You?"

"Nineteen. Major?"

"I'm still figuring it out."

She crinkles her nose and her eyes flick around the room. "Aren't you a junior?"

"Why do you do that?" I change the subject. And technically I should be a senior.

"Do what?"

"Look around like that . . . like you are always

scanning to see who's around to know if you need to impress someone or not."

She squints her dark eyes and cocks her head. Does she really not know she does that?

"Oh. I know them. They're Gregory's friends." Cheyenne reaches across the table and grabs my hand. This is so fucking ridiculous. I can't believe I agreed to play this game with her. I don't like to be used and I'm sure as hell not into fake people.

"I gotta take a leak. I'll be right back." Pushing to my feet, I head to the bathroom. The asshole's friends eye me and I wonder when we reverted back to high school.

After I get done I see Cheyenne sitting there with her arms crossed. "What happened?" I look at her friends, but they're not paying attention to us.

"Nothing. Let's just go."

Shrugging, I grab my cell off the table. Taking a quick look at my texts I see someone needs a hook up. I could walk home, but that will take too much time, so I say, "I live off campus. I need a ride home." My car wouldn't start this morning so Adrian drove me in.

"Whatever."

I follow the princess to her dorm, wondering what crawled up her ass while I was gone. She walks up to a Honda Accord which isn't what I expected from her. I would have thought she'd drive something flashier.

I give her directions to my shithole house. It doesn't take long to get there and she's silent the whole time. When she pulls over, I can tell she wants to say something. "Spit it out, Cheyenne. I'm in a hurry here."

"You're a drug dealer."

Fuck. "You know, we're not really in a relationship, so you don't need to play the controlling girlfriend card by looking through my texts." My whole body feels hot. My heart is suddenly going a million miles an hour. Who the hell does she think she is?

"I didn't mean snoop, but your phone lit up when the text came through and I caught a glance."

"It sure as hell didn't say what it was about so how do you know?"

"I just do. Ruin your life or not, I don't care. It's not my business, but if we're doing this, you have to keep it away from me. I don't want anything to do with that shit."

My whole body tenses. "Because obviously I'm doing it for the hell of it. I'm the guy with tatts who lives in the piece of shit house and gets in fights with frat boys. Obviously that means I deal drugs because I want to."

I can hardly hear through the pounding in my ears. I push the door open, get out and slam the door. The window's down so I bend over. "Everything's not always black and white, Princess. Sometimes we have to do shit because there's not another choice. Maybe you should think about that before you snub your nose at me."

Without another word, I'm gone.

CHAPTER ELEVEN

CHEYENNE

It's been two days since I talked to Colt and I'm still thinking about him. I shouldn't be. It's not like I know him very well. It's not as though this stupid charade we had going on was really making me feel any better. But I'm thinking about that last day in the car.

And thinking about how big a bitch I was.

It's obvious he needs the money. That's why he agreed with my stupid boyfriend idea. And I know his mom is dying. Dying. I could tell by the sound of his voice when he told me how much it affects him. It was the same way he spoke to me when he said he had no other choice. I'm assuming that means whatever money he's getting is somehow going to help his mom.

He's fighting for her—caring for her the way I wish my mom had cared about me.

The door opens and Andy walks inside. "Are you still moping? You're taking longer to get over this break-up than you did the first one!" She flops on my bed beside me. She's like that. Doesn't mind getting in someone's personal space and she acts like we're best friends or something.

"Want to talk about him?" she asks.

If only she knew. "No."

"You sure?" Her pink ponytail flies around as she turns.

"Yeah . . . I'm sure you want to hang out with your . . . girlfriend or something."

Andy looks like I've disappointed her. Welcome to the club, I want to tell her.

"One of these days, you're going to have to find someone to be real with, Cheyenne."

I don't have time to reply to her. As she's walking out, my cell rings. I fumble with it, not sure who I'm expecting it to be, when I see it's my aunt. "Hello."

"Hi, Cheyenne. How are you?" There's a slight edge to her voice.

"I'm okay. What's wrong?"

"It's the weekend. I wanted to see if you'd come home. I thought we could spend some time together."

My heart speeds up. Her voice is off.

"Or I could come to you. We can get a room . . . hang out. How does that sound?"

It sounds like something is seriously wrong. I fight to swallow the ball in my throat. "No . . . no. I'll come home. I need to get away anyway."

"Okay, sweetie . . . I love you."

"You, too." I don't take the time to grab any clothes. I have some at home. Purse and cell in hand, I'm out the door.

Something's wrong. I know it to the marrow of my bones. My mind flips through everything bad: my aunt and uncle divorcing, someone's sick. I don't like any of the options that squeeze their way into my subconscious. Lily and Mark are steady. The only steady I've ever known.

It only takes me forty-five minutes to make the hour drive. I see the blinds move when I pull into the driveway. It makes my gut sink even farther. I don't know how I'm as calm as I am right now.

"That was fast," Aunt Lily plasters a fake smile on her face.

"What's wrong?"

My uncle steps out of the kitchen. He's the typical wealthy workaholic—always busy, yet he's here. Why is he here?

My cell slips out of my sweaty hand and hits the floor.

Aunt Lily tries to smile at me again, but she can't quite do it. Bending over she picks up my phone.

"Just tell me." I fall onto the couch. Lily's eyes glisten before one tear slips out. They each sit on one side of me. I'm afraid my heart is going to burst out of my chest.

My aunt grabs my hand. It's shaking. Or maybe

that's hers. Or both of ours. I look almost exactly like her—her and Mom both, but there's a sadness to her I've never seen before.

"We got a visit from the police today."

Oh my God. They had to have found my mom. She must be in jail. Has she been locked up all these years? No, that's impossible. If she was, I would know. Papers were filed when she left. Everything is official and on record.

"Okay . . . where is she?" I don't know what emotion to focus on: anger or pain.

Lily starts crying harder and my uncle takes over. He shifts his weight, looking nervous. "Cheyenne . . . sweetheart. There were bones found."

My breath cuts off. My vision gets blurry. My heart stops. Bones!

"They'd been there a long time, sweetie . . . but there were teeth. They ran tests and—" He takes a step toward me, but stops as if he's unsure.

"How long?" How long, how long, how long?

"Ten years," he replies. Lily lets out a sob, but I can't manage to do anything. Ten years. Ever since she left. My mom has been dead since she left me and I didn't know. And I hated her for leaving me. Hated her for something she might not have done. Or she might have. Now I'll never know. Never know if she planned on never coming back or if something else took her away from me.

But all this time, I hated her.

"Everything's not always black and white, Princess."
Colt's words slam into me.

"I'm so sorry, kiddo," my uncle says.

My aunt, Mom's sister, clings to me. Pulls me into a hug and cries on my shoulder.

"Mommy has some things to do, Cheyenne. I'm going to bring you to see Aunt Lily. You want to see Aunt Lily, don't you?"

"No . . . I want to stay with you." I grab onto her hand. Pleading. *"I miss you when you go. I'll be good. I won't cry this time if we go out. I'll even stay by myself at home just to show you I can."*

I'll be a big girl. I won't leave the room at parties. I won't call 911 if I get scared. I won't freak out like I always do.

"Oh, sweet girl. Don't cry. You'll have fun with Aunt Lily. You can't go where Mommy's going."

I wrap my arms around her waist and cry into her belly. Cry because she's leaving me and I want nothing more than to go with her.

She didn't say she'd be back. At nine-years-old, I lost her. Not that she'd been there when I needed her two years before.

"Everything's not always black and white, Princess."
"You can't go where Mommy's going."

It could mean she knew she wasn't coming home . . . or it could have slipped her mind. Been something she thought she didn't have to tell me because I should know she'd be back.

But I never thought of it that way. I hated her.

"Do you understand what we're telling you?" my uncle asks. He looks small. It's the first time I can remember him ever looking that way and it makes me want to lose it.

I manage to pry myself away from my aunt. Still no tears. I have to hold my hands together to try and keep them from shaking though.

"She's dead. Been gone ever since she left."

She'd left before for days at a time. Even for a couple weeks. Is that an excuse for assuming the worst? That she'd planned on throwing me away and never looking back?

"The police are looking into it. They cautioned us, we'd likely never know what happened to her." Mark's voice is steadier than mine could ever hope to be.

"Where?" I manage to creak out.

"Cheyenne—" my aunt starts.

"She's old enough to know, Lily." He looks at me, no nonsense like always. "Wilsonville. In the woods."

One town over. Was she leaving? Was that on her way out of town and she got a flat tire? Someone pulled over to help? Did she go into those woods planning it on her own?

"I have to go." My chest tightens, so tight I can

hardly breathe. I yank my cell from her hand, which is hard because my fingers just want to curl.

"What! You can't leave. Not after this. I want you to stay home, Cheyenne."

"I can't." Blurry vision again. I'm somehow breathing too hard and can't get enough air at the same time. Don't panic. Not until you leave. "Someone's expecting me. I have to—I can't. I need to go."

"Wait, honey. Don't shut me out. You have to let someone in." Lily's words are close to what Andy said. They make my chest feel tighter.

I run out the door. Lily calls my name behind me. Both my aunt and uncle stand in the doorway as I rip out of the driveway. I only make it about a mile away before I hit the curb when I pull over. I hardly get the door open before I'm vomiting all over the road.

It's dark out now, no sounds besides my retching. *Bones. Woods. We'll likely never know.*

Was she alone like this? Did someone sneak up on her? Take her against her will?

I slam the door, fighting back the tears. Fighting back the panic. I put my car into drive, hit the gas and go.

CHAPTER TWELVE

COLT

"Colt. Man, that chick from the party is here for you," Adrian yells through my bedroom door.

Shit. Just what I'm not in the mood for today— dealing with the Princess. I'm a little surprised though. I didn't expect to see her again. I don't know how I feel about her being here now.

I open the door.

"I didn't want to let her in, in case you weren't alone."

"Though you didn't mind risking whoever I might be in here with knowing someone else was here for me?"

Adrian winks. "Only because party girl seems different."

"Her name is Cheyenne." I don't know why in the hell I just said that. Pushing around Adrian I head for the door. "You closed the door on her? You fucker."

A laugh is his only reply. I pull the door open. She

looks different than usual—her hair is a tied back and she's wearing faded shorts and a t-shirt. This doesn't look like the kind of clothes she'd ever let someone see her in. I don't know why, but it makes my skin feel tight.

"Back to give me more shit?" I ask, leaning my hand against the doorframe.

"No. I came to tell you it's over." Her voice cracks slightly.

"Shit," I ground out. "Let's go in my room. I don't like other people in my business."

I'm surprised when Cheyenne pushes past me. I ignore the room full of people who watch as we walk by. "Last room on the right." Once we're in, I close the door behind us.

"It's really clean in here . . . and white." She has her back to me.

"What? A guy like me can't like his shit clean?" I don't care how I look, but I like my stuff to be in order.

"The rest of the house was trashed."

"I don't have control over the rest of the house. I doubt you came here to talk about my white sheets though." I lean against the old desk in my room. Mom got for me at a yard sale, all stoked because she knew I'd need somewhere to do my homework.

"I already told you what I came here to say. It's over. The charade."

I laugh and scratch my head. "Yeah I figured that out when you got all pissed at me the other day and then didn't give me my next assignment."

Which should be a fucking blessing to me, but for some reason, I find myself annoyed about it. "You still owe me money though. I played your little game for a few days."

Cheyenne snaps her head toward me. For a second, I think she might cry, but instead she rips open her purse. "How much do you need, Colt? Is this enough?" She tosses a wad of cash at me. "Or do you want my credit card too?" The plastic rectangle bounces off the wall as she throws it. "Is there anything else I can give you? What else do you want from me!" she screams.

I have no idea what the hell is going on here, but it's obvious something's up.

"Feel free to take it all!" I dodge her purse that flies at my head. She's not crying, but it looks like she wants to. Her chest rises and falls with big surges. Something twists in my gut.

"Hey. Is it me or did we just step into the Twilight Zone or something?" I take a step toward her. The look of rage—or pain, maybe both—in her eyes slices through me. "What's wrong?" Another step.

"You mean besides the fact that my mom is dead, I didn't know and I've hated her for years? Nothing," she snaps, her voice like acid.

Those words slam into me like nothing else she could have said. Nothing else anyone could have said. My body wants to tense up and slacken at the same time. "Fuck," I run a hand through my hair. "I'm sorry."

I'm not good with words. I've never cared about it before, but in this moment, I wish I knew what else to say.

Cheyenne shrugs. "It's not like you did it. Can't change it now." Another shrug. "So yeah. I blamed her for leaving me, wanted to prove I didn't care about anyone else leaving me again, when the whole thing was a lie. Needless to say, I don't need that anymore."

Her words grate on me the wrong way. She wants them to be real, but like everything else she does, they're fake. "So . . . you're all tough then? You're just pretending this isn't a big deal? Eh, I found out my mom's dead, but I'm just going to go about my business."

"You smug son-of-a-bitch." She tries to slap me, but I grab her wrist. Like always she didn't hold back. It was a full swing. "Don't do that. You're not better than I am, hiding behind the fact that you're an asshole."

"There's a difference because I'm not in denial about it." The way her eyes dim, sad and acknowledging my words, does something to me. I feel them on me . . . in me. It's fucking ridiculous and I'm the last one who should be consoling this girl, but I grab her hand and pull her to me. "Come here."

She comes. Her arms wrap around my neck and mine around her waist. She feels small—smaller than usual, but soft and feminine tucked against me. "Life's shitty sometimes."

I expect her to cry. Wait for it. Mom's always been a crier. Real emotional about stuff, but there's no wetness seeping through my shirt from where her head rests on my shoulder.

No sniffling or shakes. Just . . . nothing.

Damn, this girl is shutdown tight. Which I should be thankful for, that way I don't have to deal with it. I find myself running my hand up and down her back though. Her grip on my neck tightens, the only sign I have she's comprehending anything.

"Your mom . . . what's wrong with her?"

Her question is a vise-grip, squeezing the life out of me. "Cancer. What else?"

"I'm sorry," she says, looking up at me.

"Me, too."

She dips her head and I know what she's going to do before she does it. Her lips brush against my neck and I squeeze her waist. Christ, this is fucking dumb. All kinds of dumb, but I don't pull away when her lips skate over my throat again.

I don't let myself think, but tilt her head up and

take her lips. I'm not slow about it either. I'm hungry, needy for her. My tongue pushes into her mouth. A little groan escapes from the back of her throat and damn it turns me on.

Her nails dig into my skin and it only spurs me on more. I kiss her deeper, studying every part of her mouth. With my lips on hers, nothing else matters, but what we're doing. I lift her up and her legs wrap around my waist. Stumbling, I walk to the bed, our mouths never parting.

Cheyenne makes a little "umpf" when we fall onto the bed, but she's still kissing and I'm still kissing her and all I can think is that I want more. I'm not stupid. I know what this is. She wants to forget about her mom and I like the way she feels and I've wanted to know how she tastes. Knowing should make me stop, but I've never really been that kind of guy, so I keep going.

My mouth slides down her neck. My tongue licking that little hollow spot I didn't realize until this second, I wanted to taste. Cheyenne's hands are in my hair as I keep kissing my way down.

I push the top of her t-shirt down, taking my tongue across the swells of her breasts. I move far enough away that I can push her shirt up this time. Her bra is satin, but still not as smooth as her skin. I cup one breast, teasing the other through the fabric.

I'm on fire. Inside and out. My hand moves to the

top of her pants. Before I go any farther, I look up at her. The heartbreak on her face—the pain in her eyes, douses my wildfire.

Fuck. What the hell am I doing? I sit up and pull away from her. I ache from wanting her so fucking bad, but I say, "We need to chill out."

If anything, my words make the darkness in her eyes worse.

Cheyenne pushes off the bed, fixing her shirt as she goes. "I gotta go."

"You don't have to." I shrug, wondering where in the hell those words came from.

"Yeah, I do." She grabs her purse. I get up and start grabbing the money and cards she threw on the ground.

"I . . ." she shakes her head.

"It's cool," I tell her. "We all lose it sometimes."

"Not me. Not anymore." Cheyenne takes the card and walks out.

CHAPTER THIRTEEN

CHEYENNE

I stay in bed most of the next day. Andy asks me what's wrong a million times, but I tell her nothing. I don't even know how to explain it if I wanted to. Which I don't. Not to her. Not to Colt, which is why I regret what I said to him, or even to myself. I was with Gregory for two years and he never saw that side of me. Never saw me lose it. Never knew how I felt about anything. I got good at the game, but somehow let my guard down with Colt. I hate it.

I want to forget. That's all. Things are never what they seem to be anyway. The past ten years of my life have been a farce that I let control me too much. Just like my relationship with Gregory had been a farce. I'm not making the same mistakes again. My eyes sting because I can't sleep. I've never really loved the dark, but now I hate it more. Was it dark for her? Did she die right away? Did—stop! I face the mirror and finish putting on my eyeliner

"How are you? Anything new with boyfriend

number two?" Andy asks. At least it's better than her questions all Saturday and Sunday.

I make myself smile because it's one of the things I can control. There are so few of them out there I plan to cling to the ones I can. "No, Colt and I broke up."

"That's too bad. He's hot. Way hotter than the other guy."

My skin suddenly tingles remembering his hands on me—his mouth. My toes curl in my sandals, but I straighten them out. He snoozed, and now he'll lose.

"Eh, he's okay."

Andy laughs. "And you're straight up lying. You know that man is better than okay."

"You should date him, if you like him so much."

"I'm spoken for, remember?"

Yeah, I do. I don't know why I said that. I turn to face her. "What's going on this weekend? Do you know?"

Andy shrugs. "I know about an off-campus party. We're planning on hitting it up. You're welcome to come if you want." She pulls off her shirt and pulls on another tee.

"Yeah, that sounds good. I need a good time." Something churns in my stomach, but I ignore it the same way I tell Aunt Lily I'm fine every time she calls.

"Nice." Andy picks up her bag and opens the door. She walks partway out, but then turns to face me. "You sure you're okay? You're all smiley, but . . . you've been tossing and turning the last two nights. When you do sleep . . . you cry."

I drop the eyeliner I forgot was in my hand. My insides tremble. My heart cracks, but I push myself into another smile. "It's fine. I got in a fight with my aunt, but everything's better now."

So now I know there are two places I can't hide: when I'm sleeping or when I'm with Colt.

The next two days pass in a fog. I laugh where I should and talk where I should. I even smile too, but none of it feels real. Lily calls so much I start to ignore her.

"Hello, Chey," Gregory says as we walk out of class.

"Hi."

He squints. "Wow. I didn't think you'd be so normal when I spoke to you."

I shrug. "I'm over it." Looking at him, I wonder why I let him get under my skin so much. Why us breaking up or him screwing Red had such a huge effect on me. I wasn't dead in the woods. All I did was lose a boyfriend.

Smiling at him, I try to keep walking. "Wait," he steps in front of me.

"I have to go. I don't want to be late for class."

But I don't go to class. I go back to my room to try and sleep before Andy gets back.

* * *

"Hey." Colt steps up next to me, while I'm walking to the coffee house on Thursday.

My heart drops off for a couple beats and then picks up again. "Hey." I keep walking and so does he.

"You ignore all your ex-boyfriends like this?"

He called a few times yesterday. I'm surprised he's trying at all. I'm not really sure why he would, but him being here is like he's picking at the edge of a sticker. Using his nail to peel back a layer of me that I can't handle removing.

"So that's how it is? I play your game and then you ignore me?"

I want to ask him why he cares. What he's going to get out of this. But then, I guess a part of me knows. We have death between us. Mine from the past and his lingering in the future. "I'm not ignoring you. I'm just in a hurry."

He stops walking. "Whatever you have to tell yourself, Princess."

I am going to kill him! I cross my arms and plant my feet. "Stop. Calling. Me. Princess."

Colt grins. It's strange because he's this tattooed, messy-haired guy who wears faded jeans and t-shirts. One look at him and you can tell he doesn't take shit—that life hasn't been easy and he's scarred because of it. But when he smiles? Really smiles, it's perfect. Like toothpaste commercial, boy-next-door beauty that makes it really hard to be pissed at him.

And I also know I just did exactly what he wanted me to do. I reacted. I don't want to react anymore, but I can't seem to help it. "Why are you doing this?"

"I'm just talkin'. What's wrong with that?"

"You know what I mean."

He shrugs and the confusion in his eyes makes me wonder if maybe he doesn't know either.

"Colt! Get the fuck over here, man. You got ten seconds or I'm leaving!" Adrian sits in car on the street.

"Bastard," Colt mumbles. "Go get your coffee. You're even pissier when you don't have caffeine."

I can't even get mad because he's smiling as he says it.

For the first time in maybe ever, when we walk away, we're not mad. One isn't stalking away from the other. We walk away separate, but together.

I have no idea whose house we're at. All I know is the music is loud, the place is packed and there's plenty of alcohol, much of which I have partaken in. The tingle of my buzz zips around inside me, taking out all of the thoughts I don't want to have.

I lost Andy a while ago, but this time I don't care. I'm dancing, drinking and not caring who or what's around me.

I feel someone slide up behind me, a hand on my waist. I turn around and Gregory is standing there.

"I don't remember saying you can touch me," I hiss.

"Aw, come on, Chey. We're just dancing."

"Where's Red?" He doesn't move his hand so I shimmy out of his reach.

Gregory's forehead wrinkles, but then he catches on. "Maxine? I'm not with her. We were just messing around. You've always been the one I want." He steps closer to me again, his mouth right up against my ear. "We're good together, honey. You know that. I screwed up, but I won't do it again."

My world is spinning, partly from alcohol, but also because of Gregory's words. I should want this. Want him. I can be normal with him and forget about Mom's body in the woods, all the tears I've cried and even about Colt. I look at him, wondering if he could make it all go away. If I can go back to pretending. Gregory smiles and my stomach aches. No, he couldn't. He hurt me, and I can't trust him. Maybe it's a male thing. Maybe none of them can be trusted.

"I have to go." I jerk away from him and weave my way through the mass of people. The music suddenly feels too loud, almost echo-y. The spins suck me in a vortex worse than I've ever felt.

"Chey! Wait."

I keep walking and so does Gregory. When he grabs my hand I try to pull away, but can't, so I keep going, dragging him with me. I need air.

"Who are you looking for, little girl? Did you lose your mama?" The man's breath stinks like alcohol and something else that I can't place. I try to pull free from his grasp, but can't.

Panic starts to pop and explode inside me, starting off like the small fireworks you do at home, but each one is bigger and bigger like the finale in New York.

Let go of me! I don't know if I say it out loud. If I'm talking to Gregory or my past. I just need out.

I fall out the door and into the yard. My chest squeezes the air, the life out of me. I try to pry my fingers open as they fist. My nails dig into the palm of my hand. "Get off me!" This time I know the words come out. I fall on the ground. Gregory falls with me. I kick and scream, trying to get away from him.

I can't see. I'm lost in a fog.

"Chey? What the hell? What's wrong with you? I just want to talk." Gregory.

I can't hold down the panic. It's taking me over, a chameleon changing me. "Go away."

"Colt!" I hear someone yell.

"I'm trying. You have my fucking shirt!" Gregory screams. There's a grunt and he's gone. I scramble to my feet, still feeling like there's a rock on my chest.

"Come with me. I'll help you find your mama." Loud music. It's still so loud.

Colt's fist flies through the air and slams into Gregory's face.

"What the fuck?! I didn't do anything to her!"

And he didn't. Not really. But I can't take it. The yard closes in on me, locking me in. Trapping me. Baring weight on top of me.

I can't stop myself. I turn and run.

CHAPTER FOURTEEN

COLT

I watch as Cheyenne's ex falls to the ground, grabbing his jaw.

"I don't give a shit what you think. You're close to her when she doesn't want you there, so you're doing something. Stay the fuck away from her."

My hand hurts. I'm breathing hard, itching for him to do something else so I can hit him again.

"You know she can't really want you, right? She's just trying to make me jealous."

Fuck if he isn't dead on, but that doesn't matter. "Think what you want, Pretty Boy. All I know is if she tells me you laid one hand on her she didn't want, I won't stop next time." Greg dusts himself off, gives me one more dirty look before walking away.

Adrian steps up beside me, so I turn to him. I look around. There are only a few people in the yard. I know she'd freak out if too many people saw. "Good lookin' out, man." He'd been outside with some chick and called for me. "Where is she?"

He nods his head. "Over there. I think she went behind that shed."

"Damage control and then meet me at the car."

I run over to the shed. Each step I take I wonder what the hell I'm doing. This girl isn't my problem. I played her little game with her and now it's over. Still, I creep around the back of the small building and when I see her huddled on the ground, I don't turn away.

"Hey . . . it's me." Fuck. She probably doesn't just recognize my voice in the dark. "Colt." I don't want her to trip out. Something serious has happened to this girl. I don't know who she is, but she's not who I thought.

"Go away."

I smirk. No matter what happens to her she still doesn't have a problem being pissed at me. "Not gonna happen."

I bend down. I'm not sure if it's the right thing to do or not, but I touch her shoulder. My hand starts to tremble from her. She's shaking like fucking crazy. "Come on. Let's get you out of here."

Another shiver wracks her whole body. It vibrates through me. Can she even walk? "I'm going to pick you up, okay? Don't kick my ass." I'm hoping for a laugh that I don't get. She doesn't tell me to go to hell either, so I figure I'm safe.

I scoop her up. Her shaky arms wrap around me. She buries her face in my neck. "Maybe you should kiss me. That way if anyone sees us they'll think you want me too much, I had to carry you so I could get you alone faster."

With that, I feel wetness on my throat. It's not from her mouth. A little whimper sneaks out of her lips and she's shaking in a different way now. She's crying and somehow I know that's a huge deal for her.

"I got you. We're good. Let's get you out of here."

I sneak her out the back gate so we don't run into anyone else. Adrian is already in his car, on the street. I manage to open the back door and get in without letting go of her. I don't have time to wonder what I'm doing or why I feel okay doing it. I can't do shit for anyone else in my life, but maybe I can help make this okay.

Adrian drives. Leaning forward I kiss the top of her head. I feel her shaking as she cries, but no sounds come out. She's locked up so tight and I both respect her for protecting herself and want to set her free at the same time. "It's okay. We're good."

"Home?" Adrian says from the driver's seat.

"Yeah."

He doesn't ask what's up and I don't offer, mostly because I have no fucking clue. Just let him drive while she cries and I kiss her head like it's a real fucking thing to do.

By the time we get to my house, her body's still. I'm pretty sure she fell asleep.

Adrian opens the car door, then lets us in the house.

When I get to my room, I lay her down in my bed, take off her shoes and pull up the white sheets and comforter she seemed to be so surprised by last time she was here. Like I thought, she's out. When I pull away and turn to walk out, she whispers, "Don't go."

Those words dart around inside me, cracking parts of my insides. "I don't belong in here with you." She's obviously got shit going on and I have nothing to give. Hell, I don't even want to give to anyone.

"Please . . . I . . ." she doesn't open her eyes, but nuzzles into my pillow. Streaks of makeup run down her face, the only sign she cried. That was huge for her. So was asking me to stay.

"Fuck." I close my bedroom door and kick off my shoes before climbing in bed with her. I pull her back to my chest and wrap my arm around her. I've held girls like this before. I'm not a saint and there have been plenty of women in my bed, but this is the first time the girl hasn't been naked. The first time I'm not just doing my duty after having sex with someone.

"Go back to sleep," I whisper. My voice is almost as shaky as her limbs were.

"Tomorrow . . . don't remind me I said this. I won't want to talk about it, but tonight . . . keep me safe."

Her words knock the air out of me like getting slammed in the chest. "You're safe with me." Which is probably the biggest fucking lie I've ever told.

*   *   *

She hasn't moved for over an hour besides her chest going up and down, her breasts pressing against her shirt. Trying to go slow so I don't wake her up, I pull my arm from around her and get out of bed.

And stand there.

Cheyenne doesn't move, so I figure I'm safe and sneak out of the room. I have to piss and my mouth is dry as hell. After taking care of my business, I head to the kitchen. Adrian's sitting at the table, his feet up and a pipe in his hand.

"Want some?" he asks.

"Nah." Pot isn't really my thing. It's a means to an end, is all. Instead of going back to my room, I fall into the other mismatched chair at our kitchen table. I don't know why. I don't really want to talk and I know Adrian will open his big mouth, but I'm sketchy about going back to Cheyenne too.

"That was pretty fuckin' intense." Adrian crosses his arms.

"No shit."

"What's wrong with her?"

I pause, trying to think of how to answer. She just found out her mom is dead, which has to be eating her alive, but there's more to it than that. More than Gregory and all the other stuff. I just don't know what it is. "Not sure." I shrug.

"Are you doing her?"

"Fuck off." Like that's any of his business.

"That's what I thought." Adrian pushes to his feet.
"What does that mean?"

He sighs and sits back down. "I don't know. You're different with her. You're feelin' her, I can tell, but not the same way it was with Deena and other girls. You wouldn't have hesitated to answer that question about anyone else. Which is cool. I'm just surprised."

I shake my head. Adrian's always like this. He smokes more weed and parties more than anyone I know, but he's never afraid to put shit out there. He has some sort of sixth sense when it comes to stuff, so I'm not shocked at all by his words. "I don't really know her, man, to be feelin' her or not."

"Doesn't change the fact that you are."

True. A guy would have to be blind not to want her. She's gorgeous with all that shiny dark brown hair and melted caramel skin. She's got pouty lips and knows how to use them. Yeah, I'd have to be crazy not to want her, but—"Things are screwed up for her. You saw her freak out and I sure as hell can't give her more than a good time. She's not the girl for that."

Adrian laughs. "You asked?"

"You know I didn't ask her."

"Then you don't know. And yeah things are messed up for her and your ass too, even though you never talk about it. Might do you both some good to find a way to forget about that for a while."

He stands and I don't plan on saying anything to get him to stay this time. He doesn't know what the hell he's talking about. She may have shit on her plate, but she's still a princess and I'm definitely not a prince. Don't want to be either.

Adrian kicks my chair to get my attention. "Plus, you'll have a whole hell of a lot of fun in the process."

I ignore him and we both walk out of the room—him toward the door and me back to my bedroom. Once I'm inside I close the door, pull my shirt over my head and toss it to the floor. Cheyenne's curled in a little ball, her hair splayed out on my pillow, her dark and it white. Like I said, a guy would have to be blind not to want her and I'm definitely not blind. We both have too much drama for it to be anything more than that.

Ready to pass out, I climb over her and into my bed. She whimpers, her body jerking slightly. On autopilot I pull her close like I did earlier. "Shh, baby. It's just me." She doesn't make another sound, but she grabs my arm. I close my eyes and go to sleep.

CHAPTER FIFTEEN

CHEYENNE

Last night plays on reverse in my mind. It starts from the feel of Colt's arm around me, flashes to the car ride, the shed, Gregory, the drinking.

My heart seizes. Oh, God. I made a fool of myself. I was such an idiot! I squeeze my eyes shut as though that will somehow make it go away, but I know it won't. It happened and there's no changing it. No changing any of the things that happen to us.

All there is to do is move on.

Starting now.

I am about to try and sneak out of the bed and save Colt and I both dealing with . . . I don't even know what. I can't say the morning after, because nothing happened besides him seeing me the way no one else ever has. The way no one should.

I try to move and his hand squeezes. It's then I realize where it is. On my breast! Holy crap. How do I get out of this one? I try to move again and this time he stirs.

"Mornin'," His voice is rough from sleep.

"Hey . . . I need to get up, but . . . ummm."

His hand jerks back. "Fuck. Sorry. Reflex."

And I know I need to thank him. To say something because what he did was huge and he didn't have to do it. Most guys wouldn't. Not after everything that's gone down between us, but instead of thank you, what comes out is, "Can I use your bathroom?"

"Sure. It's right across the hall. Are you planning on sneaking away, Cinderella?"

Getting out of the bed, I turn to him. Big mistake. Huge. He is probably the sexiest guy I've ever seen. He has his shirt off and there's that tribal tattoo on his right shoulder and leading all the way down his arm. His muscles are hard, his grin cocky. It makes me hate him a little. "From Princess to Cinderella?"

"I'm kidding. Go to the bathroom." He gets up and follows me. His pants hang low. Not too low and they're held up by a belt, but that sliver of boxer briefs shows against his belly.

"Are you planning on coming with me?"

"No, but I'd like to brush my teeth. Beer doesn't taste as good the next day."

Ugh. He's right. I stand in the hallway, letting him brush his teeth first, before he walks out.

"I'll be in bed. Just come back in when you're done."

Locking the door behind me, I fall against it. I don't feel like Cinderella. More like Dorothy in Oz. I have no idea what's going on here.

When I needed someone it was Colt who helped me.

I don't like needing help. I don't know if I like him, but he was there. He's been there. And even though I don't like it, there's something about him that pulls out my secrets. Like he's a magnet, my past, my secrets and my pain, little shards of metal unable to resist his pull. I don't understand and I don't even know if I want to, but it feels good having some of those things siphoned out.

"Stop thinking so much, Chey." I go to the bathroom, wash my hands and then rinse my mouth with mouthwash on the counter.

Running my fingers through my hair I try and make it look as though I didn't sleep like the dead last night.

Which I did. For the first night since I found out about Mom, I really slept.

Bones . . . In the woods. Gone . . .

"I'll help you find your mama."

I pull open the door, trying to leave those thoughts behind. Colt's in his bed when I get there, one arm flung over his face and the blanket up to his waist. He opens the eye that isn't covered, looks at me and then closes it again.

I stand there, not sure what to do. That isn't like me and I don't like it, but I don't even understand the space we're in right now, so I'm not sure how to navigate it.

"I don't bite . . . well, unless you want me to." Part of his mouth quirks up. "I already told you how much women like my mouth—"

"Stop! I swear you're so disgusting." But I still walk over and sit on the edge of the bed. I let a deep breath out, suck another one in. It's the only sound in the room, but I feel the burn of his eyes on me. "Thanks . . . I . . ."

Colt sighs. "Don't. You don't have to say thanks."

"You took care of me."

"So?"

I turn to him, almost needing to look away again because it's so much harder this way. "For most of my life I've never been able to count on anyone. Even when I could, I hated it. I mean, really depend on someone. Not pretend to or play it off. You saw me at my worst . . . the part of me I hate and I don't want anyone else to see, but you were there. That means something to me."

"If that was your worst, you're good. You'll be okay, Chey. I don't doubt that for a second."

I don't know why his words make me want to smile. Still, I can't make myself do it. "You called me Chey . . ."

"Eh. I had a rough night. I don't feel like fending off an attack this morning if I called you Princess."

I take him in, the blond hair that always looks like he ran his fingers through it. Those tattoos and the hard edges of his face only softened by the dimples. When I look at him, I see control. I don't know why because I don't really have it with him. We fight like crazy, but somehow I feel safe and like I have some kind of power I never knew I was missing.

"There were only a few people in the yard. Fucking potheads and people too drunk to know what the hell was really going on. Adrian talked to them though. I doubt you'll have to worry about people giving you shit."

In this moment I'm not thinking about last night. I don't care who saw or what happened. All I can concentrate on are the curve of his lips. The muscles in his abs and how they ripple.

"Shit," he lifts his hand and I'm surprised when he touches my hair. "You're really trying to kill me aren't you? You're eating me alive with your eyes." Then, he pulls me to him, his tongue gently probing my mouth. I open up and let his lips wipe away any residue of thoughts besides Colt and what he's doing to me.

"Come here," he says against my mouth and then he's kissing me again. I climb over and straddle his waist. Colt's hand weaves through my hair and rests on the back of my head, deepening our kiss. I feel his erection which makes the pressure inside me build.

His other hand slides up the back of my shirt and

even though I know it's wrong and it's not the right way to deal, each touch masks another thing I don't want to think about. When he's touching me, it's a definite, something I know. His touch is black and white when nothing else in my life is, even when I believed it to be so.

I pull away. "You make me forget. I just want to forget."

Colt flips us, so he's on top of me. My legs wrap around him and then he's kissing me again. "What do you want, Chey?" His mouth trails down my neck. "Tell me what you want."

"Control," I arch toward him. "Something I can control the outcome of. To pretend everything is okay."

"This is all I have. With—I just don't have anything else to give besides this right here." Another kiss and then he nips the lobe of my ear.

He doesn't have to say with what. I know he means his mom. That's what we have—we're both damaged with baggage and somehow it works. I never thought something like this would work for me. "That's all I want."

This time, he stops his assault with his mouth and looks at me. My breath catches.

"So we trade one charade for another?"

I smile. "Yeah . . . I guess we do."

He leans in, his mouth a breath away from mine

when a pounding comes from his bedroom door. "Colt! Get your ass out here!"

He groans. "This better be good." The muscles in his back flex as he gets up and for the first time, I notice a tattoo across his shoulders. It's another tribal spanning one shoulder to the other. Colt pulls the door open. "What?"

"You left your cell in my car last night, man. Your mom called."

"Shit," Colt rips the phone out of Adrian's hand and dials. The bed bounces when he sits back down, his leg shaking. I don't know what to do. If this was more than just a casual fling, I could wrap my arms around him. Tell him everything is fine and kiss his shoulder. That doesn't fit what we are. But he did that for me last night.

My eyes skirt over to Adrian who lifts a brow at me and nods his head toward Colt, but I still don't move.

"Hey. You okay?" Colt breaks the silence in the room.

I wait as he listens. "I'll come over." Another pause. "It's okay. I want to." More listening. "Stop arguing. I'll be there soon." Colt hangs up the phone.

"Everything cool?" Adrian asks from the doorway.

"It's alright. I need your car though."

I guess that means his is still messed up. "You can use mine if you want," I tell him.

Colt turns to me, little crinkles by his eyes almost

as though he forgot I was there. It leaves me feeling a little hollow for some reason.

"That's okay. Don't worry about it."

"Keys are in the kitchen." Adrian yawns and then walks away.

"I'll bring you back to your dorm real quick and then I need to go." He gets up, opens a drawer and starts riffling around for a shirt.

Guilt gnaws at me. What if something is wrong with his mom and he missed the call because of me? "Are you sure? If you're in a hurry, I can find another ride . . . or go with you."

His head snaps back to me at that and I know he definitely doesn't like that idea. It's on the tip of my tongue to tell him to go to hell. That if he can kiss me he shouldn't be embarrassed to have me around his mom, but then I start to get it. That's not what this is about and it feels almost too personal.

"Never mind. Scratch that last part."

Colt pulls the shirt over his head. "It's not you . . . it's just fucking weird, ya know? I mean, seeing someone you don't know like that . . ."

My mind flashes to what Mom's bones must have looked like in the woods. "Yeah . . . Yeah, I get it."

He unbuttons his pants. "Unless you want a show, you need to get out of here. I'll be ready in about two minutes and then I gotta bail."

I move toward the door, but he grabs my arm before

I can walk out. He opens his mouth, closes it again, all sorts of thoughts playing in his eyes. "We'll hook up later, yeah?"

A large breath pushes out of my lungs. "Yeah."

CHAPTER SIXTEEN

COLT

I get two texts from people who are looking to buy as I'm on my way to Mom's. I ignore them, and toss my cell in the passenger seat of Adrian's car. I'm not in the mood to deal with it right now. They'll still be there after I check on Mom.

Fuck. I can't believe I left my cell last night. I don't do that. It's always on me and I went a whole night without realizing it wasn't there.

It could have been a whole lot worse and I wouldn't have been there.

I accidentally grind the gears on Adrian's piece of shit. I'm shaking as bad as Cheyenne was last night which is completely screwed up.

I pull into Mom's apartment complex and park. Little kids are running around the place, right outside her window and I want to tell them to chill out because she might be resting, but I don't. I know she always says she likes hearing the little kids play.

"Hey. How ya doin'?" I ask when I get inside. She's

sitting in her wheelchair, in her robe even though it's warm in here.

"I told you, you didn't have to come over, Colton, but I'm glad to see you." She gives me a smile and I lean over and kiss her bald head.

"Most people are." I wonder sometimes if she knows I'm faking it with her. If she knows I'm disintegrating inside, but just don't say anything. "You shouldn't try to get out of bed by yourself, Mom."

A twenty-one-year-old shouldn't have to scold their own parent. There's something really fucked up about this situation.

"It was just a fall."

"You can't afford to hurt yourself."

She sighs. "I'm dying anyway. Sometimes, I just want to do it with a little bit of dignity. A woman should be able to get out of bed by herself."

My hands tighten into a fist. Yes, I know she's fucking dying, but that doesn't mean I want to hear her say it. It doesn't mean something wild and crazy can't happen. Cheyenne thought her mom bailed on her and she hadn't. Maybe the opposite can happen here. People get better all the time.

Which I know is a lie. It won't happen, but damn I want to pretend.

"I'm sorry. I shouldn't have said that. It's been a bad day." Mom closes her eyes and I immediately feel like shit. She doesn't have a lot of bad days. She's optimistic. The cup is half full, sunshine and flowers and I try to act like I agree, but really I'm pissed someone dumped out half of my drink.

"It's okay. It's not your fault. I was up late helping this girl last night so I'm on edge."

At that she opens her eyes and looks at me and I realize my mistake. I don't mention girls in front of her, probably because I don't do more than screw around with them. Now I brought up Cheyenne (which is fucked up in itself) and she's going to latch onto that.

Maybe I should give her something to latch on to.

I scratch that idea because we're already too tied together. Our lives are becoming too intertwined and that's the last thing either of us need right now. We're both too screwed up for that. She'll end up okay though. People like her always are.

"Is this a girl you're . . .?"

"No." I turn away from her.

"Are you sure? Why won't you look at me, Colton?"

I hear the smile in her voice and it makes me want to do the same. It isn't often she's able to give me a real one—with happiness and hope and it's about a fucking lie because there is nothing real going on with Cheyenne.

I turn to face Mom. "Because you're being ridiculous. Are you hurt? You said there's a bruise on your—"

"Stop changing the subject."

I fall onto the couch. "I'm pretty sure that's you." There's a part of me who actually wants to keep this going. It's like what we used to have. I've spent most of my life with it only being the two of us and she's always been one of those hands-on moms. If she could spend time with me—if she wasn't working, she wanted to be with me. We've always been close and it feels like that now. Like before when she wasn't bald or fell when she tried to get out of her bed alone.

I want to hold onto that.

"You like this girl!" It's the most animated I've seen her in a long ass time. She wheels the chair closer to me. "Colton . . ."

"I don't like her, Mom. Jesus, you make it sound like we're twelve."

"Who is she?"

I don't know. Who are any of us, really? Do we ever really know someone else? Hell, do we know ourselves? I can't answer that way though. "She's a friend," I shrug. Which I guess she is, which is weird as hell. "It's nothing. She's a girl from school."

And then we're both quiet and I know I somehow let her down. Or maybe that's not really it. Maybe she just wants more for me.

The smile is suddenly gone. Deep lines etch across her forehead and she looks older . . . sicker, that quickly. "I don't want you to be alone."

My heart fucking stops and my chest sinks in. I don't want to have this conversation with her. The thought makes me want to puke, hit something. Pretty much do anything rather than talk about this with her. "I'm fine."

"Colton, I know—"

"No," I shake my head at her and get up. "We're not going there, okay? I just wanted to check on you. Are you sure you're good?"

"Yes, Doctor. I'm fine. I was checked out."

I shake my head at her, but I can tell she's just having fun with me. Fun. I don't get how she can do that. How she can know what's happening and not be freaking out. Makes me feel like a pussy because she's handling it so much better than I am.

"Are you hungry? I can make us some lunch?" She doesn't eat much, but she has these shakes that she likes. Sometimes she eats light stuff, soups and shit like that.

"I'd like that."

I head to the kitchen and make us each a sandwich that I know she won't eat. There's a big pot of soup in the fridge so I warm some up for us. I eat my soup while she sips hers. She asks about my classes like she always does.

My cell blows up the whole time, but I ignore it. Hate dealing with that shit when I'm with her.

"I want a tattoo," Mom says out of the blue. I almost

choke on a noodle. She's always giving me hell about my tatts. She hates them. Thinks they're pointless so her words couldn't shock me more.

"I thought you hated tattoos."

"Things change."

Fuck. Yeah. They do. I wonder if this is one of those bucket list things. Something she's decided she had to do before she goes. "Okay," I shrug. "We'll go sometime."

"Soon," Mom says. That simple word is like a knife slicing through me, cutting me from my neck down. I suddenly don't want to take her to get a tattoo anymore. If she can't do the things on her list, she can't go. It's not right otherwise. "They say it should be something important. It's . . . something I want to take with me."

"What?" My voice cracks.

Mom smiles. "I'm not telling yet. I'm still trying to figure out the details."

I try to play her happy game the rest of lunch. Talk about charades. I give Chey shit about hers, but look at me. My whole fucking life is a game.

After lunch I clean up the mess. Her nurse walks in and smiles at me and my cell goes off again. It's an excuse, but I take it. I'm no better than my dad since I can't stay around.

"I gotta go. I have some stuff to take care of. You want me to help you into bed before I go?"

Mom yawns and I know she needs it. She gives me a small nod and I wheel her to her room. I swear she's lost even more weight. It's like picking up a kid when I put her into bed, kiss her bald head again. "No more getting out of bed by yourself. You have help for a reason."

"Yes, Doctor," she smiles again.

I walk to the door, but stop before I leave. I don't know what makes me do it, but I turn to her and say. "I'll try and bring her by, 'kay? I don't know when, but I'll see what I can do."

It's a huge fucking step and a dumb one at that. But I'll do it. For Mom, even if the whole thing with Cheyenne is a lie.

Even from across the room I see the tears in her eyes. "I can't wait to meet her, Colton."

I feel more like shit when I leave than I did when I got here.

I make a quick stop at the house and grab what I need. My gut churns the whole time. Mom would hate this part of me. Hate that I'm doing the same thing my dad did, but for me it's because I have to, not because I want to. Nothing makes this kind of money and lets me work on my own schedule so when Mom has a problem, I can be there.

I make the stops I need and get the money. I don't like people coming to our place if I can avoid it.

I think about going to Cheyenne's. I told her we'd hook up later and yeah, I want it. To lose myself in her so I don't have to think about all the other stuff, but I feel too raw. Too laid open to let her get close. To risk her getting inside.

Still, I turn away from the house and toward the dorms. I need to forget more. I know how to hold myself in check. Hell, I don't even have to try. It's no different with her.

I park the car and text her. My phone rings about three seconds later and I smile. "How you getting me in?"

"Who said you're coming in? Maybe I'm doing homework."

"I'm more fun than homework."

"You know this would be much easier if I went with you."

"Yeah, but this is more exciting." I don't know why I don't want her at my place right now. Maybe it's Adrian and his psychic-ass that'll say things I don't want to hear.

Cheyenne chuckles. "Go around the right side of the building. Toward the back, there's a door. I need to make sure the RA isn't around. I'll text you if she is. If not, the door will be open in about three minutes." She doesn't wait for me to reply before she hangs up.

I slam the door to Adrian's car and I'm halfway

around the building when I realize the buzz beneath my skin is real. The excitement, eagerness. For the first time, in a long ass time I really want something.

And I know it's the bulge behind my fly making me think this way, but it still feels pretty fucking good.

CHAPTER SEVENTEEN

CHEYENNE

I shove the picture of Mom under my mattress and jump out of bed. I didn't expect him to get a hold of me again today, but I'm glad he did. Glad I can shove the memories away and let Colt distract me.

I slip on a pair of slippers and a bra, even though I might not have it on for long, before sneaking out the door and down the hall. Thankfully the RA is nowhere in sight, but I have to steer clear of the front entrance. It's guarded like a high security prison.

My heart beats fast, and I'm not sure if it's because I'm scared of getting caught, excited to see him, or because once it's broken it goes haywire from time to time.

I ignore it all because Colt gives me something to concentrate on.

When I get to the door I eye the halls to make sure no one's around before I slide my card and the door clicks open. Colt's standing there wearing the same thing he did earlier and a smirk that mixes "Cocky Colt" and something I don't recognize.

"Don't give me that look." I shake my head.

"The look that says you got down here awful quick?"

"Who came to who?"

He shrugs. "I don't think anyone could blame me. You gonna let me in?"

"Yeah. Make sure you're quiet. If we get caught, I don't know you. You're just some creepy stalker who's following me up to my room." I turn to walk away, but Colt grabs my arm.

"Is your roommate here?"

I roll my eyes because it's a little late for him to ask me that. Colt seems to get it because he gives me another smirk and then his lips find mine. I'm squeezed between the wall and his hard body and all I can think is, damn this man can kiss.

Colt's hands move to my hips as though he's trying to hold me in place. I want to tell him I'm not going anywhere, but my mouth is too busy being devoured by his.

"I have a room for this," I'm finally able to say when his lips go to my throat.

"I couldn't wait. I've already been a saint." He pulls away and I wish I hadn't said anything at all.

The rattle of a doorknob sounds from behind us. I grab Colt's hand and turn down a hall. It's the long way, but we can still get to my room from here. The risk of getting caught is more likely, but I'm pretty sure no one besides the RA would care.

This is the only kind of situation where Colt would let me lead him around. We're not running, but walking fast and for the first time, I realize these hallways are way too long.

I turn again, before slipping into a stairwell. We're both up the stairs and then my head is out a door to make sure no one is in the hall. My room is only three doors down, so we slip out. The second we're inside his mouth finds mine again.

My instinct is to stop him. To use the hand I have on his hip and push him away. I mean, give a girl a minute. I haven't let anyone take advantage of me in a long time, but then I remember this is what I want. He's not taking advantage of anything. We both want the same thing, so instead of pushing, my hand on his hip pulls him closer.

Then he pulls away, but he's still standing so close to me I can feel every part of him. Feel his desire for me. Colt's breathing's heaving and I feel the heat of it float across my neck. I'm stuck between asking him why he stopped and feeling slightly glad he did. This is new territory. How do you move forward when your plan is just to hook-up? Do we talk? Just go for it?

Stop it!

I hate that feeling—not knowing what to do. Without knowing it, Colt saves me. "You're a dancer."

I'm wondering how he knew, but then I remember the pictures on the dresser. Me and the girls on my dance team in high school. We'd just won state.

"I am."

"Holy shit, I'm fucking around with a cheerleader." Colt laughs.

"I'm not a cheerleader, I'm a dancer. And who cares if I was?"

Colt looks at me, steps back far enough that his eyes trace every single spot on my body. I shiver.

"You're right. Why am I complaining?"

He steps closer again. So close. Holy shit, he's gorgeous. I'm smarter than to tell him that though. His jean are slightly baggy like they always are, his legs on either side of me. His hands are on my hips, the finger of his right hand teasing the skin under my shirt.

"How's your mom?" I ask. It feels right—talking to someone in a situation like this. I think. I don't want to get too close to him, but I'm actually nervous and I'm not sure how to stop it. Talk or kiss? I know which one sounds like more fun.

He tenses just a little. "I don't want to talk about my mom. Do you?"

I shake my head because he's right. Talking is overrated.

Colt pulls off his shirt, hooks one of his fingers through mine and backs up. "Which bed?"

Oh, he's good. He's definitely done this before. I laugh because had this been a different situation, if I wanted more and he wasn't so completely different from me, I could see how a girl could lose her head around him.

"Something funny?"

"The one on the right," I say rather than answer.

Colt lies on my bed and pulls me down behind him. I expect him to go for my clothes, but instead he kisses me again.

"Blanket," I mutter, between kisses.

"If you're cold I'm doing something wrong."

"What if my roommate comes home?"

"Wuss," he teases, but grabs the blanket and pulls it over us. I don't know why I needed it yet. It's not like we're undressed, but I somehow feel safer—like we're not as laid bare as we were before.

I'm not sure if I mean clothes either.

Colt pushes a hand through my hair and takes my mouth again. It's a slow exploration. Each sweep of his tongue sends little jolts of pleasure through me. They're like an eraser, wiping away all the thoughts I don't want to think about.

I'm surprised he's not just going for it. This isn't supposed to be about foreplay or anything else, but he's taking his time and I'm grateful for it. Not that I would ever admit that. And the longer he's here, the longer I don't have to think about anything else.

His hand slides up my shirt and again, I shiver. All I can think about or focus on is Colt and what I feel and it's so very much what I need. It's on my terms and it's what I want, when I want and it won't matter if I walk in on him with another girl or if he walks away or anything else.

"Sit up." His mouth is going down my body as his hands are moving my shirt up. I lean forward and Colt keeps pushing until my shirt slips over my head and lands on the floor.

His mouth nips at my breast through my bra as he uses one hand to unhook it. Pleasure bubbles inside me. I ache everywhere, but it's the kind of ache I want.

"Oh, God, I can't believe you just did that one handed. That should make me run right now."

It distracts me from the fact that he's seeing me without a shirt on for the first time. I want to cover up, but I don't have to because I'm in control and I don't freak out anymore.

"Do you want to run, Cheyenne?" I expect to hear a joke or feel his mouth, but neither happens. He's on top of me now and I look at him.

His eyes are so blue the sky has nothing on them. "No."

Then comes the smirk and he looks down at my chest. His finger brushes one of my nipples and if it didn't sound cheesy I would admit that I feel that one touch everywhere.

"What do you want?" He leans forward and his mouth takes the place of his finger on my breast. He flicks his tongue across the tip and I arch toward him.

"I don't know." I sort of hate the answer. I should know. I should be able to say, but I can't. I just want to feel and be taken away from everything else. The picture under my mattress and the nightmares keeping me awake and how I thought Gregory mattered when something that small shouldn't have had any significance on my life at all.

And suddenly, I want to cry. Why do I want to cry? I shake my head and close my eyes and will the tears away. It's not because of Colt. God, what he's doing feels so good. Maybe it's because it does feel good and I don't know if I should feel that way right now.

When his mouth stops moving, I let my eyes flutter, hoping no wetness springs free.

"This is going to give you a huge head and I'll probably regret it later, but you are so hot," he says.

He's not even looking me in the eyes. His gaze is firmly on my breasts and it's all so ridiculous and crazy and just what I needed that I can't stop myself from laughing.

Finally, he peers back up at me and the look in his eyes tells me he knows I was struggling a few minutes ago. "Should I keep going?"

When did I become so weak? I've never had to be

coddled in my whole life yet this guy I hardly know has had to do it over and over. Was there ever anyone to do it before? Or would I have accepted it?

"If you don't, I'm going to have to get angry."

Colt tsks. "We wouldn't want that."

And then his mouth is on me again. My nipples tingle at his touch. His hand moves down. Under my sweats and my panties too. I tense when his finger pushes in—the good kind of tense because it feels so good I can't handle it.

I already feel myself starting to come apart as I move with his hand. Heat scorches up my body. He was right. I'm definitely not cold. Colt's hand and mouth continue dueling out their pleasure as I bite down hard. A burst of pleasure shoots through me as he pushes another finger in. I don't want to scream, but the slow fizzle inside me is building to a bomb ready to explode at any second.

And just as it does, just as I come undone, flying higher and hit with more pleasure than I've ever felt, I start to drift my way back to Earth. As Colt's slides up my body again and I know he's moving so he can take his pants off. The door jerks open.

"Cheyenne! You'll never guess—oh. Wow. Holy shit!" Andy doesn't even turn her head.

"Andy!" I scream. Colt is on top of me and I'm covered, but I still feel my cheeks heat.

"Fuck," Colt mutters and I'm starting to read him

well enough to know what that means. This is over for now.

"You mind?" I ask, trying to play it off. "We're a little busy right now."

A smile stretches across her face and she winks. "I'm out of here." The door is almost closed before her head pops in again. "Hot. Seriously. You're way better looking than that other guy." And then she's gone.

Colt doesn't move and neither do I. Finally he says, "We're going to my house next time."

I go for trying to sound as light as he does. "Your fault. You could have called me over."

He's already moving and sitting up. He leans over the bed, grabs my shirt and hands it to me. I suddenly feel bad because I'm pretty okay and got some relief, but he didn't.

"What about . . .?"

This makes him smirk.

"Glad I'm amusing to you."

"That's nice of you to worry about my well-being, but I'm good for now. You'll owe me one." He winks and stands up, grabs his shirt and pulls it on.

Whatever. "I was getting a little bored anyway. I should do some homework."

"Bullshit." But he's smiling and I think he's having as much fun as me. If this was Gregory, we'd do our homework together. Or he'd keep going, but what I have with Colt is different. It's not about anything more than this.

"I'll call you, okay?" He looks unsure. Licks his lips and starts to bend toward me, but stops himself.

I almost tell him it's okay to kiss me, but I don't want it to look like I want him to kiss me if that's not what he wants.

"Sounds good."

With one more glance, Colt heads for the door. His hand touches the knob, but he doesn't move. I hear as he lets out a deep breath, before he turns around.

"Tell me I'm not a bastard for doing this."

He's not, but it's cool that he wonders. "You're a bastard, but not for this. No worries."

It's the right thing to say because he gives me a small nod and a smile. "Keep that. The honesty." Colt pulls the door open and steps out. "I'll see you later, Tiny Dancer."

Just like Andy, he's gone.

I can't help but think I like that name much better than Princess.

Still, the thoughts rush back in quickly. Rolling over, I pull the picture out from under my mattress and cover my head with the blanket. My mind immediately goes where it does every night. Wondering if she knew what would happen when she left me. Wondering if she wanted to leave me and what her last minutes were like.

CHAPTER EIGHTEEN

COLT

I tune out in class even more than I usually do. I come because it's important to Mom and I do the shit I need to do to get by, but that's about it. Luckily, stuff like this isn't hard for me. Are my grades the best? Nope, but they're what I need to get the scholarships and financial aid I need to keep myself locked up in this place.

And it works. The professors feel like they're doing their job. Mom believes I'm suddenly going to have this incredible life she never did because I'm on my way to a piece of paper that doesn't do anything to guarantee me a job when I'm finished. It makes her happy which makes me feel like I'm not the shittiest son in the world so it all works out.

But today, I feel like being here even less than I usually do. Christ, Cheyenne felt good the other day. The little whimpers from the back of her throat. Her body all lined against mine. I'm still trying to figure out why I pulled the breaks. Yeah her room-mate came home, but she left and there wasn't anything stopping me from staying and finishing what we started.

What my body is jonesing to finish right now, but I felt like an ass. When I'm with a girl I do it so I don't have to feel. But I was feeling and I don't like it. All those unwelcomed emotions made me bail.

But we both want it. Both want it bad so that makes my guilt even more fucked up.

When class gets over I grab my stuff and head out. My car's running for now so I head out to the lot and get in, turn it on, but don't go anywhere.

I don't know why the hell I'm sitting here, flipping my phone over in my hand. My head is all screwed up, but I don't know why, which pisses me off more.

My phone beeps and I turn it over to see a text from Cheyenne.

What's up?

Waitin on u, I text back. Which is only half a bullshit answer, but it sounds good. Today's a late day for me so it's already after three, but I don't know what her schedule is. For all I know she's not even here.

I have another hour . . . after?

My pulse jackhammers like I'm a sixteen-year-old about to get laid for the first time.

Meet u at ur dorm, is all I say and then drive my dumbass around like I have a reason to wait for her when she can drive herself.

When she walks up a little over an hour later I'm

leaning against my car waiting for her. She's back to public Cheyenne with tight jeans that probably cost more than my whole wardrobe and a shirt that shows a nice amount of cleavage.

"You coming over?" I ask, crossing my arms.

"You inviting me?" She does the same.

I hold in my smile because I don't like the fact that she makes me want to do it so often. "I just did."

She rolls her eyes. "I could have found my way to your place."

I shrug because I don't know how to reply without looking like a pussy.

"You drive me crazy," she says, but she's walking over to my car. I get back into the driver's seat and we pull away.

We're not in the car for two minutes when her cell rings. I watch as Cheyenne presses silent.

"You hungry?" I ask.

"I am, actually."

"We'll hit a drive-thru."

Her phone rings again. She silences it. After we grab our food it beeps another time. "You know I don't give a shit if that's your pretty boy, right? Play your games if you want to. We both know what this is." I tap my fingers against the steering wheel, frustrated.

"Be careful, Colt or I'll think you're jealous."

"Be careful or I'll think you want me to be."

She sighs and I'm pretty sure I pissed her off more than I wanted to.

"It's my aunt," she finally says as we pull up in front of my tiny ass house.

Fuck. And again I feel like a prick. "You don't wanna talk to her?" I kill the engine.

"Not really. She's freaking out. Thinks I'm having a hard time and wants me to come home."

I flash back to the night in the yard, seeing her all huddled in the corner behind the shed. I almost tell her she is having a hard time and that maybe she should go home, but I'm not sure it's my job. Glancing at her hands I see they're shaking slightly and her breasts are heaving against her shirt.

So I do what I'm here for. What she needs from me. I slide my hand through her hair and pull her to me. Silence her thoughts and her words with my mouth. Cheyenne kisses me greedily like she always does, like she's hungry for me and I know I'm starving for her, so I kiss her deeper. Let my other hand slide to her leg and up.

When we pull away we're both breathing hard, but I don't think she's thinking about her aunt or her mom anymore. "Damn I'm good", I tell her, which earns me a smack on the arm.

We get out and head inside. I'm not surprised to see Adrian sitting in the living room with a few people around him. Beers are on the coffee table and they're listening to music on the TV.

This place is never empty and it drives me fucking crazy.

"'Sup?" Adrian says. He sounds half asleep. "Beers in the fridge," he says and I'm about to tell him no, but then Cheyenne says thanks and heads toward the kitchen.

I fall into the chair and realize this is going to take a while.

She comes back in the room and hands me a beer, which I take, then she sits on the couch next to Adrian. It's the only empty spot. Perry and Dax are sitting on the other side of him. Perry's girl Monique comes down the hall and sits on his lap. I see Dax and Perry both eyeing Chey then me like they're trying to figure out what's going on.

I don't usually come home with girls. Deena's around, but that's just because she's always partying with everyone.

I'm really not feeling this whole thing. The hang out with Cheyenne and my friends. It makes it feel like something we're not, but I sit here and eat my food while she does the same and Adrian, suddenly awake, talks to her.

A knocks sounds from the door and I know things are about to get a whole lot worse.

I eye Adrian who doesn't move so I get up.

"Fucker." I call him as I open the door. Jack and Oscar come in.

"What the fuck's up!" Oscar yells. He's always acting like an idiot and it drives me insane.

"Beer sucks. I have Tequila." He has a brown paper bag in his hand. I close the door and keep standing.

"Damn. Who are you?" Jack says, walking up to Cheyenne.

I take a step forward to tell him to back off. To tell him she's with me, and to keep the fuck away. But I don't because she's not my anything. We don't have any promises and I don't want any so I sit back to see how she's going to handle it.

Adrian does it for her. "She's Colt's girl. Back off."

His words piss me off. Yeah I was close to saying the same thing, but she's not mine and I don't want her to be. Not completely at least. But I also don't want them trying to get with her so I don't say anything.

"Wow. Colt's girl, huh? I didn't know that." She looks at me and winks.

"Let's play strip poker." Oscar says.

Both Monique and Cheyenne shoot him down.

"Quarters?" Monique says. Neither her or Chey have said a word to each other. Girls are crazy like that, always sizing each other up and neither one wanting to talk until the other does it first.

I expect Cheyenne to say no, but she shrugs her

shoulders as if she's game. Which might not be a bad idea because I obviously need a drink to chill the hell out.

We move to the kitchen table, all of us crammed in around the thing. Monique is again on Perry's lap, her hundreds of little braids hanging down over her shoulder.

Adrian pulls out his pipe and weed and everyone around the table but me and Cheyenne smoke and then the bottles appear in the middle and we all have our glasses filled.

I don't know what makes me do it, but I lean over to her ear and nip it with my teeth. "If you get drunk, I can't have my way with you."

I watch as goosebumps blanket her bare shoulder. Damn it's hot. I want to kiss them. Trace all of them with my tongue but there's a table full of people here and I don't do shit like that. Public displays are for couples and we're not a couple. What Deena and I did we pretty much did in private. Yeah everyone knew and I didn't care, but I also didn't go around whispering shit in her ear.

I lean back in my chair to give us some space.

Cheyenne turns to me and smiles. "Don't worry. I'll be good."

I want to tell her I don't want her to be good. Instead I lean forward and add a little more tequila to my glass.

*   *   *

I am so fucked up. I don't remember the last time I drank so much, but one game led to another. It was crazy watching Cheyenne with my friends. They're so different but she was laughing her ass off the whole night and her and Adrian kept sharing these looks that if I wanted more than just to get her into bed, I'd be pissed about.

Everyone just left and I lean against the kitchen counter and crook my finger. "Come here," I say.

Cheyenne steps between my legs and I'm dizzy as hell, but I still manage to kiss her. She tastes like tequila and my body is yelling, finally, at me because this is what I've wanted all night, but then I have to grip the counter to keep myself standing up.

"You are so trashed. Didn't you tell me not to get too drunk?" She smiling, but I don't feel like smiling. I try to kiss her again, but she backs up. "You're too messed up, Colt. I should go."

"Give me a few minutes and I'll be good."

She pauses for a few seconds before she says, "I should go."

But she doesn't sound like she wants to go and I sure as hell don't want her to go, so I hook my finger in the loop on her jeans and start toward my room. She's laughing, but following me. I slam the door behind us, take off my shirt, kick off my shoes and step out of my jeans.

"I just need a few minutes." The room is spinning.

Why the hell did I drink this much? I climb into bed in my boxer-briefs and lean on my elbow and watch her. "Are you scared, Tiny Dancer?" I ask.

Like I knew she would she toes her shoes off. I watch as her jeans come next and she's standing there in these bright purple panties against her caramel skin.

"I'd ask if you had something I could wear, but that feels too official, doesn't it? Me wearing your clothes?" She smirks. At least I think she does.

"You won't need clothes."

She shrugs, turns out the light and slips into bed with me.

"Just a few minutes," I tell her again. I close my eyes to keep the room still. Feel her against me. "You gotta do me a favor." My lips are against her neck. I lick her skin there just because I need to taste her.

"What's that?" She sounds sleepy. Or maybe it's me. I don't know.

What was the favor? "My mom." I try to kiss her neck again, but don't have the energy. My brain is telling me to shut the hell up, but my drunken self doesn't listen. "I need you to go see her with me."

Cheyenne's quiet for a few seconds. I'm too messed up to worry about it.

"Sure . . . yeah. Okay. I can do that."

And then nothing.

CHAPTER NINETEEN

CHEYENNE

My sleep is unbroken for only the second time since I found out about Mom. It feels good to get a full night. Not to be chased and plagued by nightmares that make me feel weak. Of memories I can't change, and questions I'll probably never have answers to.

I can't believe Colt asked me to go see his mom. I wonder if he meant it. If it will be one of those things people say when they're too drunk to know better, and try to forget afterward. It's what I'm assuming. I don't know how I feel about it either way so in some aspects, it would be easier if he forgets.

It felt good to be asked though. I wonder why he did. I know it couldn't have been something he wanted, which means somehow his mom knows about me. What did he tell her? That I'm the reason he was late the other day? Some messed up girl he's messing around with?

But not really. I'm the girl he's supposed to be

having fun with, but we really haven't done much.

Colt's hand grips my waist and squeezes. Not too tight, but strong enough that I know he's there. That he's awake. My heart speeds up and I breathe harder.

"No more games. I want you," he says into my ear. His breath is warm. His whole body is as he molds against my back. I feel his erection as he nudges against me.

"Roll over, Cheyenne."

I do what he says and his mouth comes down on mine. It's more urgent and needy than all our other kisses combined.

"I thought beer didn't taste good the next day?" I ask when his mouth moves down to my neck.

"No time." Colt licks my collarbone and then sucks my flesh into this mouth. I moan and arch toward him.

He's putting up the barriers again. I know it, but I don't care. We need them there so both of us remember exactly what this is about.

So both of us are able to forget.

Colt pushes my shirt up and I lift so he can get it over my head. I want it gone. Nothing between us because his hands feel so good on me. When he touches me I don't think of anything else. Don't feel anything else and all I need is that reprieve.

My bra comes next. I don't have time to feel embarrassed because his hot, wet mouth covers my nipple and again all there is, is Colt.

I tighten a hand in his hair, fisting it, not sure if I'm trying to pull him closer because I need more or push him away because it's too much.

He groans. From my pulling his hair or because I feel as good to him or he does to me, I don't know and I don't care. I let my other hand slide down the smooth plane of his back, under his boxer-briefs and cup him.

"Fuck," he rasps and moves against my center. He curses too much and I want to tell him, but I don't think I can form words right now. He's so hard, nudged between my legs and rubbing me just right.

And then he's gone and I miss the weight on top of me. Colt's looking down at me with those blue, blue eyes, his hair even more tousled then I've ever seen it.

"Are you sure?" he confirms. I almost smile because he asked. He's so hard and rough, but he has this caring side I don't know if he realizes is there.

I'm not sure it's a good thing that it's there, so I say, "I'm smart enough to know what I want."

Without a word he climbs off the bed. I watch the sinewy muscles of his back move as he walks to his dresser, opens the top drawer and pulls out a condom.

Nerves suddenly sneak their way in. I've only ever been with Gregory. I only planned to be with him because we worked and he gave me what I needed, but now, even though I know more than anything I want Colt, it scares me.

Maybe the fact that I want him so much is what freaks me out.

I reach for the blanket, but he tsks at me. "Don't do that. You're not shy, Tiny Dancer." And that easily, he pushes his boxer-briefs down. No shame, not that he has anything to be shameful about, but he bares himself physically so easily. Maybe it's because the rest of him is so shut away.

Colt climbs over me on the bed. I don't know what emotion to focus on: passion or nerves, but then he's pulling my panties down my legs.

And he's rolling the condom on.

When his lips kiss my lower stomach, passion wins out. Then his mouth finds mine.

He's pushing in and I'm crying out, my nails in his back, my mind shut off.

Yes, my mind is shut off, but my body is definitely on.

Colt starts to move and I move with him. It hurts slightly, but his lips on my mouth and his hand on my breast helps to dull the pain. Both physical ache and the one weighing heavily on my chest that's been there since I found out about Mom.

Maybe longer.

Neither of us says a word as Colt gets up to get rid of the condom.

Not a word when he climbs back into bed.

Not a word while we lie there . . . and lie there.

The nerves are back, topped off with awkwardness. If this was Gregory, he would have passed out holding me. Colt's eyes are open and so are mine, his right arm and my left arm the only part of us touching.

"I should probably get going. I have some stuff to take care of." Despite my words. I don't move.

"Okay. Yeah, whenever you want, I can bring you back."

I get up and start to get dressed. I hate putting the same thing on two days in a row and can't wait to get back to the dorm to change. But still, I will him to say something. Anything. I don't need him to ask me to stay, but some kind of anything would help calm the storm in my stomach.

Colt sits on the edge of the bed, grabs my shirt and hands it to me. I pull it on, telling him I have to go to the restroom and leave before he can get up.

I splash water on my face, hoping it can wash away the past few weeks of my life. When I look in the mirror, it's all still there. I'm still there.

But I feel okay. The first time I slept with Gregory I freaked out. Went to the bathroom, sat on the floor and had a panic attack he never knew about. He didn't know about any of them. Once I calmed down I washed my face like I just did here and went back into the room smiling.

It feels good not to have to smile if I don't want to.

Colt's standing in his room when I get there. He's wearing a pair of long, cargo shorts and a t-shirt. It shouldn't look as gorgeous on him as it does.

He picks up sunglasses and slips them on. It's the first time I've seen him wear them and can't stop myself from asking, "Had a little too much to drink last night?"

"I'm cool." His voice sounds distant. I'm sure he's like this with every girl he sleeps with. I don't know why I didn't really expect it with us. I don't know if I care or not. I definitely shouldn't care.

I shake my head and walk out of the room. I'm not dealing with this. It's supposed to be easy and if he's going to be a jerk afterward, it's not worth it.

Colt follows me out and we're quiet for the ten minute drive to my dorm.

"Let me know . . . about your mom." I reach for the handle as he pulls into the lot.

The only reply I get is a nod of his head. Again, whatever.

I open the door, get out and close it. We're supposed to be old enough to sleep together without it being awkward the next day. Especially when I can tell that's what he does—sleeps with people he never plans on being serious about.

I'm almost to the steps when I hear him yell, "Chey!" I turn and Colt's standing outside the driver's door looking at me.

Seconds pass by and he doesn't say anything.

"Tick tock," I say.

"Did it help?" His words come out unsure.

The tightness in my shoulders evaporates. I let out a deep breath and suddenly know we'll be okay. That whatever it is—this charade we're playing is still intact.

"Yeah . . . yeah it did. You?"

Then he smiles. It's not a huge one and I can't see well enough to know if his dimple is showing.

"Yep." Colt climbs back into his car and then he's gone.

I chuckle as I go inside. Smile again when I walk into my room. I'm not there for a minute before my phone rings.

One glance takes the smile from my face. I know I can't keep ignoring her.

"Hey," I say to Aunt Lily when I pick up the phone.

"Cheyenne! I've been so worried about you. Don't avoid me like that anymore. I know it's hard . . . but we have to stick together."

And I know what she's saying. She's Mom's sister. I'm her daughter. We're all that's left of her. I hate how I'm treating her, but can't seem to stop either. Can't let her in.

My hand tightens around my phone.

"I won't."

"I'm worried about you."

"I'm fine." Am I?

Aunt Lily sighs. "We want to have a service for her, Cheyenne."

"What!?" I pace the room. My heart has a seizure and my chest tightens. Don't freak out, don't freak out, don't freak out.

Why is this even a surprise? I should have expected it. It's normal, but . . .

"She deserves it. I want to say goodbye."

Does she deserve it? Yes she does, but then she left me. She still left me and it was so normal for her that we didn't think twice about her never coming back. What if she went in those woods and killed herself?

"I . . ."

"It will be good for us, Cheyenne. I want a place to go see her. She's been alone all this time." Lily's voice cracks. "She was my baby sister." The pain in her voice stabs into me.

She was my mom. What's wrong with me?

"I know. I'm sorry. Let's do it."

The words come out, but I don't mean them. If I tell her goodbye, that means she'll really be gone.

CHAPTER TWENTY

COLT

I can't fucking believe I'm doing this.

I'm sitting outside Cheyenne's dorm, waiting for her to come down so we can go see my mom. My fucking mom. Adrian's only met her in person once. I don't do this, but Mom's been driving me crazy about it for the past three days. I can't disappoint her over something as small as this.

Cheyenne and I are already playing the game. What's adding another level to it? Another lie we can both play and pretend is really a good idea. I'm not stupid. I know it's not, but I know when I touch her it takes me away and I really fucking need a mental break. To lose myself in her heat.

"Hey," she says from behind me. I stand up and turn. Damn, she's hot. Her legs are firm and now I know it's because she danced. Of course she's wearing a skirt because she may not realize it, but in some ways she really is a princess.

Heat scorches beneath my skin and I want to forget everything, take her back to her room and strip her.

"Let's go back to your room." I take a step toward her, almost touch her but stop. This situation we're in is so screwed up because it's a lie and I don't know how to act around her.

Fuck it. I let my hand slide under her shirt and grip her waist. "It'll be a lot more fun to stay here," I say against her ear.

"Colt." It sounds like a warning, but she leans her head to the side to give me better access to her neck. I dip my tongue in the hollow spot behind her ear.

"Let's go." I pull her against me and let her feel the reaction my body has to her.

"Your mom is expecting us."

I kiss a trail to her mouth. "No . . . I didn't tell her yet. I figured I'd call on the way."

This makes her tense and I'm sure it's going to be one of those things girls make a big ass deal of when it really doesn't matter. "Don't do that. Come on." I try to persuade her.

"You were taking me to meet your mom and you didn't even tell her yet?"

Groaning, I pull away. "It's not a big deal. I was going to call her before we went."

"No. You never planned on going. You may think you did, but you didn't."

"I—" Don't have an answer. I shouldn't have to have one. "You're acting like a girlfriend."

She pushes me away. "You're acting like a prick."

Cheyenne tries to walk away, but I grab her wrist. She's fucking right and I know it. "Wait." And she does. Doesn't turn around and I don't speak right away. Finally I man the hell up and say, "This isn't easy."

Cheyenne turns and I can see it in her eyes. She gets it. It's crazy how much this girl gets me. I don't pretend to understand it or want to.

"But it's important."

I give a short nod. "I'll call her in the car."

We get in her car and I pull out my phone and call Mom. It takes a while for her to answer, but she always does.

"Hello?" her voice sounds raspy.

"Hey. I'm heading over. I have—I have Cheyenne with me. I just wanted to make sure you were home and not running around town."

I hope for a laugh and get one. "I love you," she says and I'm not sure why.

"I love you too, Mom. You're good? If you want me to come alone—"

"—I don't think so," she interrupts me. "You're not getting out of this, Colton. I can't wait to meet her." I'm not surprised when she hangs up.

"We're good," I tell Cheyenne and she starts the car. I give her directions to Mom's place, my leg bouncing up and down the whole time. She didn't sound good. When does she ever sound good? Am I doing the right thing or being the biggest fucking fraud in the world by lying to my dying mom about Cheyenne?

I glance over at her. She looks nervous too and I realize she probably has shit going on right now that I've been too big a prick to think about. "You good?"

She nods. I recognize it as the one I give when I'm really not cool at all. "This means a lot to me." It's the best way I can think to say thanks.

"I know."

"Did you talk to your aunt?"

Cheyenne looks at me and gives me that smile I know knocks guys on their asses all the time. "This isn't about me."

"I'd rather it be."

"I know that too."

We pull up at Mom's old apartment complex. "She doesn't look good."

"More things I already know."

I can't help but crack a smile. "And you say I'm an asshole." I pause for a few seconds. "You know she's going to think you're my girl, right? That she's going to be gushing all over you because I've never brought anyone home and all she wants is—" I can't finish the rest.

"I know."

I feel like a pussy because I'm actually cracking up here, but Cheyenne leans forward and kisses me. I lose my head to her like always, biting at her lip and sucking her tongue into my mouth. Christ, I want this girl. More than I've ever wanted anyone else.

Too soon she pulls away.

We get out of the car and I lead her to the apartment. "Looks like I'm the one asking you to play the game this time," I say to her before opening the door.

Mom's sitting in her wheelchair by the window when we get there. She has a hat on which she doesn't do much anymore and I know it's because of Chey. I fucking hate she has to meet the first girl I've ever brought home dying and with no hair.

I hate that I'm a fucking liar and it's not even real.

My gut aches. I try not to breathe through my nose as we go inside.

"Hey, Mom. I found this girl outside. Do you know her?" I point at Cheyenne, who smacks my arm.

Mom shrieks, "Colton!" And I want to curse the name. How could I have spaced that?

My hand itches to grab Cheyenne's. I don't know if it's because I'm cracking up here or because I want to play the part. It's not something Mom would expect though, so I don't.

"Mom, this is Cheyenne. Chey, this is my mom, Bev."

"It's very nice to meet you." Cheyenne holds her hand out for my mom who shakes it.

"It's nice to meet you too." Then she looks at me. "She's gorgeous. What's she doing with you?"

We all laugh. Cheyenne's and Mom's feel a lot more real than mine. I keep seeing her through Cheyenne's eyes, this frail, dying woman, like that's all she ever was. She doesn't know the woman who used to work her ass off every day. The one who tried to get me to play every sport she could even though we couldn't afford it, or kept going with no sleep after graveyard shifts at work to be there whenever I needed her.

The woman who loved to laugh and always told jokes and has a temper that makes her a good weapon to have on your side.

"Please, have a seat, Cheyenne." Mom speaks softly, but I can tell she's trying not to. Trying to sound normal.

"You don't have to pretend to be nice to Cheyenne. She gives me hell all the time. She's only showing you her good side."

Cheyenne laughs and grabs my sides like she's going to tickle me. I have no clue what she's thinking because I'm definitely not ticklish, but still, I grab her arms and pull her toward me. Now she has her arms wrapped around my waist and we're chest to chest. She's laughing and I almost want to laugh with her. For a second it feels real and okay. The knot in my gut loosens and I'm not scared to breathe.

When I hear my mom sniff, I look down and see her eyes wet. I jerk away from Cheyenne and lean down. "Hey. Are you okay? Did something happen?" It doesn't even matter that there's fucking panic in my voice and Cheyenne is right here.

Mom looks at me. Touches my hair. My cheek. And smiles.

"Everything's perfect, Colton."

No. Everything's a fucking game.

We're driving back home and I can't get the visit out of my head. Mom and Cheyenne were all fucking chummy and laughing. She stayed up longer than she has in a long time. She even got Cheyenne's phone number, which I have to admit, I don't like too much.

Which makes me feel like an ass, but I *am* an ass so might as well embrace it.

Toward the end she looked tired—so fucking tired she fell asleep the second I helped her back into bed. She's lost more weight, her body feels so small, like a twig that if you step on will break in half.

"Come home with me." The words weren't planned, but I'm glad they came out.

"Your car—"

"Fuck my car."

Cheyenne doesn't reply, but she goes to my place instead of the dorm. It's actually quiet when we get there. As far as I can tell, Adrian's not even home, which is a huge shocker. The second the door's closed I'm on her. Kissing her, my body tight against hers as I wedge her between myself and the wall.

Cheyenne's hand tightens in my hair and she wraps her legs around my waist. I'm so hard, I'm not sure I can wait. I want her. I need her. My mouth doesn't come off hers as I stumble down the hall with her in my arms. I kick the door closed behind me and slip a hand under her skirt.

Yeah I like her skirts. Easy access. And from the feel of things, she wants me just as much as I want her.

I lay her on the bed and clothes are coming off. There's no talking. No laughing. Nothing but eager hands and sad eyes.

She's so fucking sexy, all smooth skin and feminine curves. As screwed up as it is, I try to avoid her eyes. Don't want her to look in mine either. Just want to feel her heat wrapped around me instead of the cold pain we both feel.

I grab a condom from my pants and rip it open with my teeth. I don't want to think about or feel anything, but Cheyenne.

She's lying sideways on the bed. I put my hands flat on the mattress, one on either side of her head.

And we don't move. She's beneath me and I'm leaning over her and I want to push home, but I can't move. Why the fuck can't I move?

Her hand slides up, wraps around my neck and threads through my hair. That's all I need. My eyes don't leave hers and hers mine as I push inside. Just being inside her makes me forget everything else. She feels so fucking good. Suddenly, my eyes can't leave hers as I move, doing what both of us need me to do.

"I should go . . ." Cheyenne's next to me, my arm slung around her. Hell it's hasn't been ten minutes since we finished.

"Yeah?" I kiss her shoulder, letting her know I'm up for another round if she is.

"Yeah," she replies, so I ease away from her. I don't hide the fact that I'm enjoying the view as she gets dressed. She's gorgeous. She knows it. I know it. I'm not going to pretend she isn't.

"What about your car?" she asks.

I shrug. The piece of shit doesn't matter anyway. "I'll have Adrian take me to get it."

"I can pick you up."

"I'll call you."

She stands there for a second, arms crossed, eyes searching everything in my room but me.

"What is it?" I ask. She still looks nervous. "I just showed you the most painful thing in my life. I think our lines have pretty much been shot to hell, don't you think?"

I sit up. Naked.

"They're having a service for my mom."

"Fuck," I say. I knew something was up, but she played it off all day. For me. For Mom.

I reach for her, but she shakes her head.

"Can you go with me? We're getting together at my aunt's house after. Food. People. Gregory's family will be there."

I have to hold back not to say something about him, but I don't. She was fucking incredible with my mom today and I can do this for her.

"Yeah. It's cool. I'll go." I'm shocked that it bothers me she won't let me hold her. That's what I'm here for. To make her forget, the way she does for me. It's all I can do.

"Thanks . . . I . . . thanks. I'll text you the information."

She walks out of my bedroom. I let out a breath and fall backward on the bed. I have no idea what the hell we're doing here or even how it happened.

My door opening makes me look up. I grab a pillow to cover the goods, but it's Cheyenne.

"You're a good son, Colt. You . . . you're incredible to her. I just wanted you to know that."

This time, she's gone for good, but she doesn't leave my thoughts. And for the first time I admit to myself, I don't want her to go.

CHAPTER TWENTY-ONE

CHEYENNE

No one here even knew who she was. I wonder if I really did. If Aunt Lily really did. If Mom knew herself.

Do I know who I am?

The only people here who can claim to pretend to know who Mom was are me, Aunt Lily, my uncle, and cousin. Otherwise it's my aunt and uncle's friends. Not a lot of them because most couldn't be bothered and the ones who are here probably only came out of respect to Lily.

But Gregory's here. His family. Of course Lily and Mark's best friends would be here. They stand on the other side of the black coffin. I don't even understand having a coffin since all she is, is bones, but I know Lily wants the best for her. She always wanted more for Mom than Mom wanted for herself.

Colt is next to me wearing nice black slacks and a button-up, long-sleeved black shirt. I wonder if he went out to buy the clothes or if he had them. Not that it matters, but I know him and this isn't the kind of thing he's comfortable in so I'm grateful he's doing it for me. I'm also thankful he didn't do his hair. It still looks like it always does, sticking every which way.

His grip on my hand tightens, but I don't squeeze back. I'm glad he's here. Hate admitting it, but I need him here. My body is just too numb to do anything about it.

The remains of my mother's bones are in a box as dark as the nights she spent in those woods. How much of her can even be left?

The pastor goes on and on. I don't focus on what he says, just the feel of Colt's rough hand holding mine. This rough boy who hates the world, curses like a sailor, but is so gentle with his mom and is here with me.

I don't understand how we got here or why we're in this together, but I'm not sure I could get through this day without him.

Something else I don't like to admit.

My chest tightens again.

Calm down, Chey.

"You're doing fucking awesome," Colt whispers in my ear and I can't help but smile at that. Only he would use the word 'fuck' at my mom's funeral.

The service ends and they have me walk forward first to toss the rose in. Colt stays attached to my side.

I feel the eyes of everyone else on me, watching me, waiting to see if I'm going to break down. Inside I have. I'm all cracked apart, pieces lying here and there throughout, but for some reason, it can't escape. It's like there's a roadblock keeping it in and while I'm glad, I want to be free of it too.

Once the roses are tossed in, we turn around. I keep walking so Colt keeps walking, supporting me as we head back to the blackened car. I can't believe they rented a car to come in. Mom didn't give a shit about stuff like that. Though she didn't give a shit about anything except partying and guys.

Colt leans against the car and pulls me toward him. My arms go around his neck and his around my waist. My face is in his neck and I think if I was going to cry, this would be the perfect place to do it, yet it doesn't come.

"You're so fucking tough," he squeezes my waist like he always does. "I just—I see."

It's then the enormity of what I did hits me. I asked him to come to a funeral for my mom, while his is dying. He looks at that box and sees Bev, but he's here and he's holding me, this boy who I'm only sleeping with.

"I'm sorry."

"No reason to be." Colt shrugs. But there is.

My aunt and uncle get to the car. They're taking the Colt thing better than I thought. Not that they're the kind to freak out, but I've never mentioned him. Didn't even tell them he was coming with me. It makes me feel bad. They would love me, if I'd let them.

Lily pulls me away from Colt and hugs me. She's crying so much my dress gets wet, but I still can't push them out.

My uncle mumbles something to Colt and Colt replies.

Everyone is walking to their cars now and I just want to get away. Want a minute to myself which I can't even have because we're sharing a car with my aunt and uncle.

Colt and I slide in the back and them in the front. They try for small talk with Colt—asking about college, how we met, how long we've dated and thanking him for coming. He speaks as little as possible. He's not one of those boys who's good with someone's parents, or in my case, my aunt and uncle.

For some reason, the house feels like there are more people here than there were at the service. Funny how that happens. People who can't make it to the sad part want to come in when the wine is offered freely and it's more like a party.

"Show me your room," comes from behind me in that husky, cocky voice I recognize as Colt's.

Thank God.

People talk and walk paying no attention to the only daughter of the dead woman. Maybe it's because she's been dead for ten years and other people saw this coming even though I didn't.

Once we're up the stairs I keep my finger hooked with his and lead him into my room.

"Holy shit. It's . . . happy in here." I hear the laugh in his voice.

"What's wrong with wanting happy?" I ask, looking around the room. Flowers are painted on the walls at the top. Each of the four walls a different color. Dance trophies and pictures of my dance team are everywhere. It's perfect, like I always wanted.

Colt looks at the bed. "It's white." He grins.

"I guess that means you have good taste."

He goes from one wall to the next, looking— dissecting. I can't stop myself from wondering how it looks through his eyes. If the room feels like me or if he thinks it's a lie.

"You must be good, huh?" He touches one of the trophies.

"Of course."

He shakes his head. "Of course."

And then he steps up to me. His mouth finds mine. It's a gentle kiss, slow and smooth as his tongue slides between my lips. I let him lead and I follow because right now it's easier than thinking about anything.

Colt doesn't stop kissing me. Our tongues tangle and take turns, but he doesn't take it any further. When he pulls away I'm panting. My heart races. Every time he touches me I want him more.

"You don't cry, Tiny Dancer." His chin rests on the top of my head as we hold each other.

"Not if I can stop it."

"It's okay, you know."

"Wow. Is the hard-ass going to give me a pep talk?" I feel like a bitch the second the words come out, but he doesn't call me on it.

"I don't know if pep is the right word." Then he leans closer. "Just know that you can. I won't tell. I might not be able to do much for you, but I'll hold your secrets."

My breath catches. It's the most amazing thing he's said to me. Maybe that anyone has ever said to me. Still, it means so much more coming from him.

"I—"

"—Chey?" The door pushes open and Gregory's there.

Colt tenses against me.

"Is there a reason you're coming into my bedroom?" I ask Gregory.

He's not looking at me though. His eyes are hard on Colt. "This is her mom's service, if you didn't notice. You could wait to take advantage of her until later, don't you think?"

I swear I feel Colt's body overheat. "Jealous I can take care of her better than you? It's okay, Pretty Boy, I've kicked your ass more than once, it's only natural I steal your girl too."

Colt's words feel like a slap across my face. I know they're just to piss Gregory off, but they hit every button inside me that I don't like pressed.

"Fuck you." Gregory steps into the room and Colt moves toward him.

"Excuse me? You didn't steal me from anyone." I'm shaking now. Colt doesn't turn around to look at me. Gregory pretends I'm not there too.

"Why don't you get out of here so we can finish where we left off?" Colt says. "I don't feel like fucking with you today."

There's a fist around my throat, tightening and tightening. I don't know why I'm freaking out, but I hate the things Colt is saying, hate that Gregory is here and then the coffin—that big black box her bones are probably lost in flashes through my head.

I gasp. Colt and Gregory are muffled voices in the background. I turn away from them, not wanting to let myself lose it. Why am I losing it? My vision blurs. I can't catch my breath. *Bones. Coffin.*

My feet tangle and then arms are there. The door slams and I'm on the floor in someone's lap.

"Shh. It's okay. Relax. You're good. We're good."

A hand runs through my hair. Lips press to my forehead.

"You're good. I fucked up. I shouldn't have done that shit today. Take a deep breath."

I fight through the panic, following Colt's voice.

I find his blue eyes. His sad lips. Gregory.

I struggle to get out of Colt's hold.

"He's gone. I locked the door. It's okay."

Now I'm back to me and the spell is broken. I get out of his lap and stand up. I open my mouth to tell him not to treat me like a game of tug-o-war, but he stops me. "I'm not good at this stuff. I don't do this stuff. I react and that's what I did. It was the wrong thing to do."

I can't say anything to his apology, because I know this isn't what he signed up for but he's here and he's doing it and it's not like I'm perfect either.

"It's not even him as much as what you said. Don't do it again." I straighten my clothes and finger comb my hair. "We better go downstairs."

Colt stops me before I can walk away. "Do you take anything? For the panic attacks?"

I shake my head. Not anymore. "I don't need medication. I've handled them for years. I'd be fine if everyone would just leave me the hell alone."

But I'm not fine. He's not fine either.

We make it through the rest of the day. Colt is

always there, but we don't touch. It's not the same as it was before the freak out.

When I pull up in front of his house, I sit there, not sure what to do.

"Come in with me," he says. He didn't ask and I'm grateful for it.

I turn off the car and go inside. We head straight for Colt's room.

"I hate this dress," I say when we get to his room. He opens his drawer and tosses a t-shirt at me. I'm so shocked I almost miss it.

Colt starts to undress first. He lies his slacks on a chair and then his shirt. I figure I need to start doing the same thing so I take my dress off, pantyhose and then slip on his shirt.

What are we doing? Usually he's undressing me, not giving me clothes to wear.

"Hit the light, would ya?" he says before climbing into bed in camo boxer-briefs.

"You're camouflaged. How will I find you?" I tease and he cracks a smile.

"I don't think you can miss me."

I turn off the light and get into bed wearing my panties and Colt's t-shirt. I wait for him to kiss me. Or to lick or bite my neck. He likes using his tongue and teeth.

Instead he pulls me to him, my back to his chest.

His arm goes around my waist and it fits so perfectly there.

"I fucked up," he says again. "That shouldn't have gone down earlier."

His words aren't expected, but somehow they're what I need. "I know. It's okay." Pause, and then, "I can't believe she's gone."

Colt squeezes me tighter. Kisses my hair. "It's easier to hide in the dark . . . but easier to let go too."

And I know he's hiding. Doesn't want me to see him when he says stuff like that. Can't be that close. Me? I'm letting go. Finally, a tear slips from my eye. I wipe it away and go to sleep.

CHAPTER TWENTY-TWO

COLT

I'm sitting in the passenger seat of Cheyenne's car messing with the stereo. It's the first day I've seen her since her mom's service and I'm really fucking hoping we're not going to have this huge ass conversation like girls like to have. Yeah she stayed and yeah we didn't have sex. We both know what happened—or that nothing happened. The end.

"You have shitty music," I tell her. When I resort to the radio, you know my options are limited.

She shrugs. "I'm not all that into music."

This surprises me. "You dance."

"Yeah and I listen to music for dancing. When music is on I'm thinking about my body and how to move and it makes me want to do more than just sit around."

I look at her and grin. "I'm thinking about your body and how it moves too."

She quickly glances at me. "I'm kind of impossible not to think about."

I laugh because it's true and she's probably the only woman I know who would have the balls to say it.

"Or touch." I reach over and slide my hand up her leg. Unfortunately she's wearing jeans, but I let my hand creep higher.

"You're distracting me."

"That's the point." I never expected to have fun with her like this. I don't have fun with anyone like this, but just like it's hard not to think about her body, it's hard not to enjoy her too. Yeah she pisses me off, but that kind of makes it better.

And then because we're almost to the party and it's only been a few days since she buried her mom, I ask. "You sure you're cool with going out?"

Again she looks over at me. I can't see her real well because it's dark, but I know her eyes are on me. "Why Colt, one would think you're a nice guy."

Her comment annoys me a little. Not because I think I'm this nice guy, but because she's always deflecting shit. She's had a lot go down lately. I've seen her when she breaks and know she's not doing as well as she wants people to think. Or maybe as good as she thinks.

But fuck. That's what I'm supposed to be. A distraction. I knew that going into it and know it now so I don't know what the hell my problem is with it. Maybe it's because I'm in the same boat.

"We both know I'm not a nice guy. And we both know there's a lot of shit in your head too. That's why

I'm asking. If you don't want to answer, tell me you don't. Don't play me."

"I don't want to answer." We're quiet for a few minutes. I'm feeling way more pissed than I have a right to be. Finally she speaks. "It's hard. I'm trying to deal. Distractions help. Fun helps. You . . . help." The last part I can tell she didn't want to say.

Did I want to hear it? I don't know. "Good."

"How's your mom?"

Fuck. Why did I start this? I just gave her shit so it's not like I can't answer her now. "The same . . . how else? There's nowhere to go, but down."

"You never—"

"You saw her, Chey. There's no hope. She stopped treatment. Hospice has been involved. We both know what's going to happen." The words hurt coming out. I want to close my mouth. Trap them in, but it won't make things any different.

Now it's her hand that's on my leg. "So . . . tonight . . . When we get home . . . Do you wanna?" There's laughter in her voice.

"Fuck yeah, I wanna."

We pull up at the house for the party. It's out of the way and on property and I can see the bonfire out back already.

I'm about to open the door when Chey asks, "What's the deal with you and Gregory?"

I hit the interior light. "He's a prick?"

"Nice try."

I shrug. "That's basically it. I fucking hate guys like him. Thinks he can get away with whatever he wants. We were out one night and we caught him fucking around with this kid. It was bullshit frat stuff, but they had the kid shitting his pants he was so scared. Him and his friends were making him go in and steal something. They threatened him. We kicked his ass. He didn't like having his ass kicked and I liked doing it."

When my eyes hit hers she has that lost girl look. No, not the lost look, but the one that says she's thinking all sorts of things women don't usually think when looking at me. "Don't do that. It's not a big deal," I say.

She gets a huge smile on her face. A cocky one that says I'm not going to like what she says.

"Don't worry, Colt. I won't tell anyone that you're really quite noble."

She gets out of the car and slams the door, giving me no choice but to get out with her.

We're sitting around a big ass fire, beer in hand. There's about forty people out here. More in the house. None of Cheyenne's pretty boys, so it's more kickback than the frat parties on campus.

She's sitting on my lap, my arm wrapped round her waist. Adrian's sitting next to me with whatever girl he's boning this week. He keeps giving me that look like he did in the kitchen that night. Like he knows or feels something else going on than is really here.

"Shut the fuck up," I say when he winks at me.

"Huh?" Cheyenne asks.

"Nothing." I bite her shoulder softly instead of playing Adrian's game.

"Ah, so you're the new flavor of the week. He's good, isn't he?" I look up to see Deena standing in front of us. I really didn't want to do this shit and hoped she wasn't here. I know she doesn't want me. She just wanted to screw around like I did, but I also know she's the kind of girl who wants to be on top. Who wants to show everyone she doesn't give a shit and that she's going to use Cheyenne to do it.

"Who are—" Cheyenne says at the same time I say, "Deena."

I feel Chey tense, but she doesn't move off my lap.

"Stop playing games, D. No one wants to hear it." Adrian laughs beside me.

"She can't speak for herself?" Deena adds.

I know this can't end well. Deena's not one to back down and Cheyenne doesn't take people's shit.

"Actually she can," Chey says. "And maybe you were only around for a week, but I've been here longer than that. It doesn't look like I'm going anywhere anytime soon, either."

I see the shock register on Deena's face. She didn't expect Cheyenne to fight back. She looks like the tiny dancer she is. Looks like the princess I've accused her of being. That's what Deena expected.

"Good for you." Deena grasps for something to say, but just stands there.

"Did you need something else? We're a little busy here."

"Bitch," Deena mumbles before walking away.

I bury my face in Cheyenne's hair knowing I'll probably regret this later, but my buzz doesn't seem to care. "You want to stick around, huh?"

Cheyenne laughs and says. "Well, you have your uses. She was right. You are pretty good and I like your mouth."

She turns on my lap, straddling me. Her arms go around my neck and her lips find mine. I'm scared as hell I might want her to stick around too.

Adrian nudges my shoulder a while later.

"What's up, lover boy?"

"Fuck off," I tell him. I rip my eyes away from Cheyenne as she talks to her roommate on the other side of the fire. Why the hell I'm standing here and watching her, I don't know.

"You're different." Adrian takes a pull from his cigarette.

"Why do you do that? Want to read my palm too?"

He puts the cigarette out and pushes it into a beer can. "I'm not psychic and don't think I am. I just pay attention to shit. I'm not afraid to say it either. You act like an asshole and I tell it how it is." He shrugs and walks away.

I push every thought out of my head and get back to watching my Tiny Dancer.

CHAPTER TWENTY-THREE

CHEYENNE

I wake up naked and in Colt's arms. It's becoming a habit—a planned one, but one all the same. His hand is latched onto my breast like it always is. I think he'd surgically attach it if he could. I don't get guys and their obsession with boobs. Not that I have huge ones, but I still struggle with guys talking to my chest instead of my face.

Colt moves behind me and I can tell by the change in his breathing that he's waking up. He shifts, his hand tightens and I know he's really awake.

"Even in your sleep all you think about is sex," I tease.

"Can you blame me? I'm good at it," he nudges a knee between my legs. I moan. It feels so good, but I have stuff I need to do. Plus, I'm not sure if we're supposed to do the morning after thing. We usually don't. I always leave.

"I can't." I jump out of the bed before he can change my mind. He looks all rumpled and sexy and

I want nothing more than to climb back into bed with the jerk.

"I'll be right back." I pull on his shirt and a pair of shorts before heading to the bathroom. I see bodies lying in the living room. This place is always packed with people. I know it's Adrian and not Colt, but it still gets frustrating.

I go to the bathroom and then brush my teeth with the toothbrush I hid here. When I head back into the room, Colt looks like he's already passed out again. The guy can sleep more than anyone I know. His school schedule isn't full time, but I wonder sometimes if he ever goes.

"I should go . . . I have homework to do." I grab my bag so I can get into my own clothes. I probably should have done that from the beginning, but there's something hot about wearing a guy's clothes that makes a girl feel sexy . . . Loved. Not that I want to be loved by him or anyone else, but still.

Colt opens his eyes. He shrugs like what's he's about to say isn't a big deal, but the nerves in my stomach tell me it is.

"So do it here. I have some to do too."

Something happens inside my chest. I've been really good at keeping him at arm's length so far. We're nothing alike. I think he hates me half the time and we don't belong together. We're a means to an end, but with his simple request, I begin to soften inside.

It's that stupid girl heart-pounding, hearts-floating-by-my-head thing. Where the guy who fights so hard to keep the distance, does something so small, it's huge. I can't help but let it inside. Let it mean something.

I should leave. Run right now because Colt and I wouldn't work. It wouldn't be like it was with Gregory. He could really hurt me—not just wound my pride.

"Don't. You're looking at me funny. Don't do that, Tiny Dancer." His voice isn't angry at all. It almost sounds confused. "It's just homework. I had my mouth on you . . . I was inside you last night. Don't make a big deal out of nothing."

I roll my eyes, trying to play it off. "I didn't do anything. Sounds like you're the one making it a big deal. Do you want me to fall for you, Colt?" I want to tease him and call him Colton like his mom does, but any kind of joking that has to do with her doesn't feel right.

He doesn't answer my question, but says, "Is your stuff in your car?"

"Yeah. I'll run and get it."

Colt shakes his head. "I'll go. I'm sure the house is packed with passed-out assholes."

Again my insides soften to him. Another simple gesture, but again something really sweet.

Sitting on the bed, I take in the view while Colt gets dressed. I can tell he knows I'm watching, but I also know he's cocky enough to get off on it. He only slips on a pair of sweats and no shirt before he disappears. He's gone for about five minutes so I assume he went to clean up too. When he gets back in the room, Colt closes the door and tosses me my backpack.

"Do you need the computer?" he asks.

Computer? I didn't even know he had one. "No. I have to write a paper, but I have to do first drafts with pen and paper."

"You're fucking crazy." He winks as he speaks, then grabs a set of keys and unlocks a box in the closet, before pulling out a laptop.

"You lock up your computer."

"You've seen the parties here, right?"

I don't know why, but that makes me laugh. Colt shakes his head at me as I continue to giggle, but he's smiling too.

"That's crazy," I say between laughs.

"I thought we just decided you were crazy." Then he adds, "Seriously though. You never know what people will do when they're fucked up. I'm cool with most of the people who party here but alcohol and drugs make people do stupid shit."

This makes me freeze. *Loud music, Mom gone. I'll help you find your mama.*

A shudder takes me over.

"Hey. What's wrong?" Colt reaches over and twirls a lock of my hair around his finger. It's so sweet, so normal that I want to lean into him for support. To tell him everything I didn't tell Gregory in years of going out with him.

I want him to protect me like he's done so often, but that freaks me out too. I can't risk needing anyone . . . but I almost feel like I need him.

"Nothing. Just a chill."

He's had to pick me up too many times. That's not what we're supposed to be about and whatever this thing is between us, I don't want it to end.

"A chill my ass." But he doesn't call me on it, only turns on his laptop and gets to work. I do the same. We work in silence for a good hour, but I'm so aware of him. Of how he smells like man and fabric softener. It's funny because his clothes are wrinkled half the time and he doesn't care what he wears, but he always smells so . . . clean.

I look over at him, his forehead creased as he reads something on the screen and I think about how comfortable this is. How easy and normal and I can't remember if I ever felt this way with Gregory. Actually I know I didn't.

This is a game. Our game. One that I asked for, but with each day it feels more real. More real than anything ever has and I'm not sure how I feel about that. What to do. I shouldn't fall for this guy. He's got so much on his plate and he's not the kind of guy to really fall for someone. Gregory was, and look how that turned out.

I turn back to my paper.

But I do. I think I like him and part of me wants to like him while the other thinks I should stuff everything in my backpack and never come back.

When you like someone you trust them and I've never trusted anyone in my whole life. How can I pick Colt?

Something jabs me in the side and I jump. "Holy shit." I look at Colt who has a pencil in his hand, close to my back. "You scared the crap out of me."

"Where the hell were you? You sure as shit weren't here." He's grinning. I love that grin so much. It's so boy-ish. Such a contradiction to his dirty mouth and bad attitude.

"I was so lost in thought about you that I couldn't handle it. I mean, I'm sitting here with Colt. How can I not feel totally enamored?"

He looks at me almost confused for a second before saying, "It's about time you realized that."

And then his laptop is gone and my books and notebook shoved to the floor and Colt's on me.

My clothes are gone in no time and then his. His mouth is on mine and he's fumbling with a condom. His tongue moves to the peak of my breast and I cry out before he pushes inside.

It's not because of how I feel right now or how well we move together. It's about *him*. Us. I know that it's no longer just an empty thought. It's the truth.

I'm falling for Colt.

*   *   *

Colt's sitting in the car with me as we head to the coffee house. I'm in major need of caffeine and even though I know he doesn't drink coffee and I'm going back to my dorm after this, he insisted on going with me.

His phone goes off for what feels like the millionth time and I realize what's happening. He's meeting someone to sell them weed. It had nothing to do with me.

Anger simmers beneath my skin. I don't think I have the right, but I hate seeing him do this. Know he doesn't want to, but then I think about his mom and know some of the money goes to help her.

Can I really blame him?

We pull up in front and I turn off the car, look at him and without thinking say, "I can help."

Colt pushes his cell into his pocket. "Help with what?"

"Money." I shrug. "Whatever you need."

Colt groans and drops his head back. "I don't need you to save me, Princess."

The name hurts. I don't want to be his princess. That's the name he called the girl he hated.

"Fuck you, Colt." I reach for the door handle, but he touches my other arm.

"I'm not trying to be an asshole."

"Then don't," I throw back at him.

"I can handle it."

I sigh and touch his hand on my arm. Thread our fingers together half expecting him to pull away or me to pull away, but neither of us do.

"I hate that you have to."

He sighs, his answer surprising me. "Just like I hate the fucking demons you have locked inside you that you won't tell me about. The ones you only let out when you can't control it and you panic. We can't always control what we don't like, Tiny Dancer."

That name makes me exhale a breath. "But I can do something to help you." And don't you know you already help me?

Colt flinches. "She hardly gets enough to take care of what she needs. If she's in a lot of pain, she runs out. She's dying, Cheyenne, and if she wants to run the air conditioner every day all summer because she's hot or if one of the only times she can eat she craves lobster and filet mignon, I want her to have it. She wants nothing but for me to be in that stupid fucking school and I don't always get all the money I need. It's not like I'm doing it because I want to. I fucking hate the shit. My dad sold drugs. Her mom was a crackhead. Do you think I want to feed that shitty habit?"

My heart breaks for him—calls to him. I want to open it up and lock him inside.

But then, he can get a job too. Selling weed isn't the only way to make money.

I know what it is, know he doesn't expect to be any more than he is, than his dad was, so he plays the part. Following the path he thinks is set for him. "You're better than that."

And before he can get frustrated or before he can storm off, I crawl to his lap and kiss him. My hand slides through his messy hair and he grips my sides so tight it's like he's afraid I'll slip away.

"You're not a princess." He leans his forehead against mine.

Those words do more for me than I want to admit.

His cell goes off again. "I gotta go, baby."

Colt's hand slides down my face and he kisses me quickly. I sigh, but climb off him and we each get out of the car. Colt walks over, hand on my hip like always and kisses me again. "You are so fucking hot."

A wink. And then he's gone.

Andy walks over to me. I didn't even see where she came from.

"It's pretty sad when the only time I see my room-mate is when I run into her at a party or the coffee house."

I shrug.

"You should see the way he watches you. Didn't take his eyes off you the whole time we talked at the party. It's cute. He's hot. We should double date sometime."

Her words make me sad and I keep watching Colt

as he gets farther and farther away. "It's not real. It's a game."

"It looks real to me," Andy replies. "Maybe you don't see it or don't want to, but it's real. Looks to me like you finally found your person to be real with. Maybe sometime you'll let me in too."

Just like Colt, she walks away from me.

Scary as it is, I hope she's right about Colt. Maybe even about her too.

CHAPTER TWENTY-FOUR

COLT

I've never really felt like an upstanding guy. Especially when I'm taking money from someone and giving them drugs, but I feel even more like shit after my talk with Chey.

I try not to think about it as I make the guy drive me back home. One of the people I was supposed to meet didn't show. I should have taken my own fucking car. I don't know why I even rode with Cheyenne to the coffee house.

Without going in the house, I stuff the extra baggie in my trunk. I jump in my piece-of-shit and head to my mom's. It wasn't planned to go over there, but I need to see her.

"Hey. I didn't expect to see you today." She gives me a weak smile as I walk in.

"I couldn't stay away." I give her a kiss and then sit on the arm of the couch. "How you doing today?"

It's dark purple under her eyes and her lips are cracked from being so chapped.

"I'm good. How are you?"

Instead of answering her I say, "You look dehydrated. Are you drinking enough?" I get up to go into the kitchen, but her sigh stops me.

"It's hard to hold it down."

My heart seizes. "Water?"

"Yeah . . . It's been a couple hours since I tried some. Maybe a few sips."

She's only doing it for me. I hope like hell it doesn't make her sick because I know she needs it.

I head to the kitchen and get her a small glass of ice water and then another cup filled with only ice.

"Do you want to suck on an ice cube instead?" It's probably a stupid fucking thing to ask, but it makes sense to me.

"Yeah, that might help." She reaches a shaky hand toward me and I try not to flinch. "Maggie had me do that earlier."

That's good. Maybe it's not so stupid then.

She sucks on the ice cube for a few minutes and we're silent. I can't stop myself from watching her even though it's actually the last place my eyes want to be. Seeing her like that makes me want to empty everything in my stomach. Makes my chest fucking ache like someone's embedded a knife there and won't stop twisting it.

"I think I need to lie down. Do you want to go and talk to me in there?"

I nod, her words shoving the knife deeper.

Once I lift her frail body into the bed, I sit next to her. She grabs my hand and it's so small. So thin I feel like I might break it if I tighten my grip. I want to spend as much time with her as I can, but I almost feel guilty too. Like I wear her out. It's hard to always see her in bed or put her there.

"What are you really doing here today, Colton?" She rolls to her side and looks up at me. She looks tired. So fucking tired.

"What? I can't come see you whenever I want? I'm here almost every day."

She gives me a look that says I should have the answer to that question. "I'm your mama. I know all." Another small smile. "Your eyes are a million miles away. What's going on in that head of yours?"

Christ, I know it makes me sound like a pussy, but all I can wonder is how the hell I'm supposed to get by without her. What the purpose is to keep going if people as good as her have such a shitty life. The only thing she has to count for it is me and how sad is that? I'm in college, though I hate it. It's my third year and I'm still taking gen-ed classes, not sure what to even do. I'm a drug dealer, drink too much, have a bad mouth and am screwing a girl who just lost her mom, while trying to pretend I'm doing it for her when it's really just because she feels so damn good.

When I don't answer she continues. "You should

see how that girl looks at you. I'm glad I got to witness it."

Her words couldn't make me feel any more like shit because Chey and I aren't even serious. Are we?

"It's not what you think."

"Or maybe you don't want to admit it," Mom counters.

I try not to argue with her because she's good as hell at it, even during times like this when I know she's wrong.

"All I want in this world is for you to be happy, Colton. You deserve it and I know you think you don't, but you do. If she can make you happy, you grab onto that. You grab her and never let go."

My eyes actually start to fucking sting. Happy. What the hell is that? Can Chey make me happy? Am I happy now? Is it happiness when I laugh with her? Push inside her?

"I . . ." Nothing else comes out though.

Mom squeezes my hand with more strength than I would think she had. "I still want my tattoo, you know? I expect you to get it for me."

My chest loosens slightly at the change of subject. "You don't want a tattoo. I know you don't."

"Maybe I used to not, but I do now."

I shake my head at her. I can't imagine trying to get her into a tattoo parlor or her sitting there while someone gave her ink.

"I need to go." I push to my feet, fully aware there was no point in this visit.

"Okay. I'm glad you came to see me."

"Me too." I give her a kiss and then walk to the door. I hear Maggie in the other room, so I know she's not here alone. "I'll see you soon, okay?"

I turn to look at her.

"Are you happy, Colton?" she asks. "I know I'm sick and it's hard . . . but are you happy?"

My throat is squeezed so tight I don't know if I can answer her. Such a simple fucking question, but I don't have a reply. Not one that I really feel.

I squeeze the door handle. "Yeah, Mom. Of course I'm happy."

My heart jackhammers as I drive through town. I don't know where I'm going or what I'm doing, I just know I need to get away. I head to the outskirts of town, this little ghetto park hidden in the middle of nowhere that no one uses.

And pace.

I fucking pace and I don't know why. I just hear Cheyenne telling me I'm better than what I do and Mom asking if I'm happy. All she fucking wants is for me to be happy and I can't even give her the truth on that.

But I want to. For the first time I realize I want it for her and I want it for me. I don't want to be that piece of shit pot dealer who leaves his girl to sell drugs. I don't want to have mom look at me like I'm her favorite person in the fucking world, but know she wants more for me than what I'm doing too. She knows. She has to know what I do or who I am.

My phone buzzes. One look tells me it's someone wanting weed. The phone flies out of my hand, against a tree and busts apart. Busts in a million pieces like I'm doing right now.

Tears fall down my face and I hate that, but at the same time hope they can cleanse me. Somehow absolve me from my sins.

I feel like nothing. I don't know who I am or what I want, but I keep pushing through with my shitty ass attitude while my dying mom hopes for more for me.

Do I ever feel like anything?

Yeah, when I'm with her. Or with Cheyenne. Holding her or kissing her or protecting her from the demons in her head.

I want that. I can't believe I want her. Really want her, but what do I have to offer?

I let loose. Scream and I know it's crazy. Hell maybe I am cracking up, but I try and let it all out of me. Push it out because I'm tired of fucking feeling this way.

I want her. I want something. I don't know what, but I don't want this, standing in the middle of nowhere and cracking up.

I'm tired. So fucking tired of fighting it and feeling this way—whatever the hell way it is. I lie about everything. I'm a dick to everyone. I can't even truthfully answer the question "are you happy?". But she sees more in me. They both do.

My feet start to carry me back to the car. I don't know where I'm going or what I plan to do when I get there.

Actually, I do.

I'm going to Cheyenne. I need her.

I'm not a block down the street when I see the red and blue flashing lights in my rearview window. All I can think about is the weed in the trunk of my car.

CHAPTER TWENTY-FIVE

CHEYENNE

My phone rings a couple hours after Colt leaves. I fumble for it thinking it's either him or Aunt Lily (who is still blowing up my phone), but see a number I don't recognize. I almost put the phone back down, but something makes me answer it. "Hello?"

"Cheyenne?"

I recognize the voice instantly. I jump up out of bed. "Bev. What's wrong? Are you okay? Is it Colt?"

She chuckles and it sounds like a sicker, more feminine version of Colt. It makes me sad and smile at the same time.

"No, no. Nothing's wrong. Unless you count the fact that I'm dying."

My heart stops. Words completely lost. How do I reply to that?

"Not today, though. Today I want you to do a favor for me."

My breathing picks back up again. "Absolutely. Anything."

Happiness sprouts inside me. I'm honored she would come to me and I don't even know what she wants. The woman has only met me once, yet when Colt is obviously unavailable, she comes to me.

"I want to get a tattoo."

I stumble. That wasn't what I expected at all. "Umm . . . okay?"

Another laugh and it may sound ridiculous, but I already miss Bev. I can't imagine being Colt and knowing I'm going to lose her. It was different with my mom and I still can't get over it. We weren't close and she forgot about me more than she thought about me, but your parent is always your parent. Colt has this loving, awesome woman as his mom and he's watching her wither away.

"I know it sounds crazy . . . especially given all the trouble I've given Colton over them. Our biggest argument we ever had was when he came home with his first tattoo at seventeen."

I sit on the bed, hoping she'll tell me the story.

"Thinks he's big and tough that one, but he knew I would be pissed. That's why he got it on his back. Tried to hide it. He may think he's good at lot of things, but getting something by me isn't one of them. I know my son and I knew the minute he came home that he'd done something he knew I wouldn't like."

"What happened?" I find myself asking.

"Well at first I didn't know what it was, but I could tell he was nervous. He may think he is, but he's not a good liar. I spent the evening watching him and I noticed him flinch when he leaned against the back of the couch. Don't tell him I told you, but he's not real good with pain either."

I laugh, thinking of a younger Colt trying to hide a tattoo from Bev. "How did you figure it out?"

"Walked right over to him, made him stand and pulled his shirt up, of course."

This makes me laugh harder. Soon Bev joins in, but then starts to cough. I can tell she's out of breath. "Are you okay?"

She sighs. "Okay as I'll ever be. Cheyenne . . . I want to do this. I feel the need to do it and I don't want to wait."

Two things hit me. First, if she doesn't want to wait, she doesn't think she has much time. My chest feels empty at the thought and my eyes begin to sting.

And second. Colt doesn't approve. That's why she's coming to me. There's no other reason that makes sense.

"Bev . . ."

"Please. Do you know how it feels to be a grown woman and have to beg for help for something like this? I want it. I need it and Colt is stubborn. I think . . ." her voice cracks and I think she might be crying.

"I think he somehow thinks I'll get better. That I

won't be sick anymore and I'll regret it. I know I'm
not getting better, Cheyenne and I want this."

I'm crying too now. How is Colt going to handle
losing her? He won't have anyone left.

He'll have me.

Not that I know if he even wants me.

"You can't leave. I can't risk taking you out of the
house."

The silence on the other side of the phone tells
me she thinks it's a lost cause.

"That's what Maggie said. What's the difference?
I'm dying anyway."

Those words are the answer I need. They confirm
the only decision I can make right now. It helps
knowing her nurse is okay with it. "I'll make it happen,
okay? Don't worry. I'll do this for you."

I hang up the phone, scared to death helping Bev
is going to make me lose Colt. This isn't my place.
She's not my mom, but she came to me as a friend.
I know what it's like to need someone and not have
anyone there. I won't let Bev feel that way.

It's going to cost me a lot of money to get this tattoo
artist to go to Bev. I can't even tell them what kind
of tattoo she wants or anything, but I find a girl willing
to go.

She lost a grandma to cancer.

"I lost my mom too," I tell her. It's so crazy. It's

the first time I've said the words that way. Said them at all except for the first time I told Colt. They hurt— prick and prod at my insides, but not as much as I thought they would. It' slowly becoming okay. Well, not okay, but a part of me. Real.

Tammy gives me a sad smile as she packs up all her tattooing equipment.

She follows me over to Bev's. On the way, I try to call Colt. No answer again. It's the third time I've tried. He's going to be pissed, but I want to at least tell him what I'm doing.

"Thank you, so much," I tell Tammy as I lead her toward the building.

"No problem," the tattooed, pierced woman says.

I knock and Maggie answers the door. She startles a little at the two of us. "Bev called and asked me to come over."

"Does Colton know?" she asks.

"No. But she wants it. He'll understand." I lie. Or I don't. I don't know. I think he'll get it. It's just a tattoo, but if what Bev said is right then I get what it means to him. If she won't have the chance to regret it, it means she's really dying.

Oh God.

I suddenly feel dizzy. My chest starts to tighten. Am I doing the right thing?

I fight back the panic threatening to take me over. "Can we come in?"

Maggie nods and steps back. We walk around the woman and into the hallway. "She's in her bedroom."

"Is she sleeping?" I ask.

"No. Now I see why." Maggie smiles and I feel a little bit better.

"This is okay?" What if something I do hurts her?

As if she knows where my thoughts are going, Maggie grabs my hand. "It's not going to hurt her. A lot of people do things like this toward the end. It's a way to honor their living and feel like she's keeping him with her.

Him.

It has to do with Colt.

Stupid tears threaten to come again. I don't know why the hell I'm crying so much.

Would my mom have gotten a tattoo for me if she knew she was dying?

Is it selfish of me to wonder that right now?

Maggie leads us to Bev's room. She's sitting up in bed, a hat on her bald head. My heart seizes seeing her. She's so sick, it's surprising she can even sit up right now.

"Hey." I walk over and give her a hug. I don't know if it's the right thing to do, but I know I can't imagine doing anything else. "This is Tammy. She's going to give you some ink." I wink, trying to sound light.

Tammy looks nervous as she shakes Bev's hand. "Nice to meet you. Do you know what you want?"

Bev nods. Tears almost come again when she tells Tammy what she wants. The tattoo artist smiles and starts to prepare her equipment. I watch as she opens all new packages—even new paper towels and cloth. She sets out ink and cleaner, explaining she only brought a few colors.

That's okay, Bev tells her. She only needs black.

I hold Bev's left hand while Tammy tattoos her right wrist. She doesn't flinch at all, sits there, strong eyes glued to Tammy while she works. I can't stop myself from looking at her. I bet she was beautiful. I'm sure her hair was blonde like Colt's. He has her smile. The dimple I love, though I think hers is deeper. Because she's so skinny or if it was always that way, I don't know.

I see pride simmering off her while Tammy works. See how happy she is. How honored she is to be doing this for her boy.

For Colt.

I think she might be the most incredible mom in the world. This woman who has been through so much, but she's still here. My mom who hadn't been through nearly as much, but wasn't.

Both gone or dying too early, one with nothing to repent, but suddenly I'm angry. Angry about my mom and so honored by Colt's.

Funny . . . I'm not mad at her though. For her. Because she missed seeing me the way Bev sees Colt.

Because she was taken when she still had so many years to change. What if she'd changed?

"All done." Tammy's gloves snap as she removes them. Bev doesn't move. Doesn't speak. For a second I'm afraid I did the wrong thing. That she does regret it or Tammy did something wrong, but then she looks up at me. Tears glittering from her purple ringed eyes and I know those tears aren't of regret. They're of love and happiness.

"It's beautiful." Bev tries to smile between her tears.

She's not my mom and I hardly know her, but I hug her. Tight. Hug her like my mom had hugged me the last time I saw her. Did that mean she knew she would never see me again? Right now, it doesn't matter. Nothing does besides Bev and love for her son and the look of pride on her face.

I hug her so tight I'm afraid I'll break her, but I can see she knows she's done something today. To her, no matter how small this is, it's something huge for her. Now Colt isn't only a part of her heart, but he's engraved into her skin too.

"Thank you so much for helping me do this," she whispers in my ear.

"Absolutely. I'm glad I could."

I pull away and see that Tammy isn't in the room. I'm wiping tears and Bev's wiping tears.

"How much do I owe her?" she asks and I shake my head.

"Don't worry about it—"

"No—"

It's the least I can do. For her. For Colt. "Please. Don't worry about it."

Bev squeezes my hand. "I'm tired. I need to rest." Her eyes are already fluttering closed.

"Okay. We'll tell Maggie how to care for it. She'll have to come in and wrap it," I tell her, not sure she even heard me. When I'm a couple steps from the bed, her voice stops me.

"I'm glad he has you."

I leave before I break down in front of her. He does have me. I only wish I knew if he wanted me or not.

Tammy's waiting for me when I get to the living room. "How much do I owe you?"

A tattooed hand wipes a tear away on her own face. "Nothing. Nothing at all."

I can't sleep. Andy's snoring in the bed next to mine. The room is dark, my cell phone gripped tightly in my hand. I've called Colt a million times today and no answer. We left each other earlier. I called before and after the tattoo. Nothing.

I would try Adrian, but I don't have his number. Would go over there, but don't know if that's too, "stalker-girlfriend." He doesn't have to call me. There's no rule, but he usually does or we're together.

I roll over in the bed, knowing sleep won't come. Knowing if I try, dreams of Mom dying, of being in the dark or of Bev's sick face will haunt me.

So I lay here and let my thoughts haunt me instead.

Rolling over, I pull the picture from under the mattress holding it in the opposite hand as my phone. Willing one to ring and needing the other close.

I'm exhausted the next day. I tossed and turned all night. Every time my eyes closed the dreams would come making them jerk open again.

I try Colt five more times. No answer.

Fear seeps its way into me. No, it's been there since last night, but now it's multiplying.

I take a quick shower and dress. Go to class though I don't feel like it. Keep trying Colt's phone and don't get an answer.

It's a long day at school and it's late afternoon by the time I'm done. I need to check on Bev.

I need to find Colt.

I drive by the house. Adrian answers the door and says he hasn't seen him since yesterday. I check his room to make sure. My heart is going crazy now, begging me to let the panic take over.

Bones in the woods.

She's gone.

I'll help you find your mama.

I start to feel dizzy. What if something happened to him? What if he's hurt or alone like Mom was?

"Whoa. You okay?" Adrian grabs my arm, but I jerk away. I can't have hands on me right now.

"I have to go. Call me if you find him." I rattle my number off to him.

I concentrate on my breathing as I drive to Bev's. Get it together, get it together, get it together. I can't scare her. Maybe he went to her house. Maybe he's mad at me. There are a million possibilities and the last thing I need to do is scare her.

I knock on the door and Maggie answers again. "Is Colt here?" I ask.

"No. I haven't seen him since yesterday before you came over."

I hold my breath so she can't tell I'm breathing so hard. He's fine.

Bones in the woods.

"Can I check on Bev?" I fight my voice to keep it steady.

"Sure. She's in her room resting."

Maggie lets me in and I go straight for Bev's room. I don't pause before slipping in the open room. It will give me more time to freak out.

"Hi." Don't scare her. "I just wanted to check on your tattoo."

She holds out her wrist proudly. "It looks amazing."

I want to touch it, but know it will hurt. "Are you putting the cream on?"

"Maggie has been."

I'm holding her wrist and looking at the tattoo when I hear a noise behind me. I turn, relief flooding the length of my body.

Colt.

CHAPTER TWENTY-SIX

COLT

"What the fuck is that?" It's a stupid question, but it's what comes out of my mouth. It's obvious it's a fucking tattoo, but what I don't understand is why it's on Mom's wrist and why Cheyenne is here with her.

Here.

With my mom.

Without me.

"Colton! Watch your language!" Mom sounds more pissed than I've heard her in a long time. I like it because it almost sounds normal. Like she's okay, but one look at her reminds me she's not.

My eyes find her wrist again and I take a few steps forward before I freeze. My name on her wrist. She put my name in her skin.

Because she's dying. Because she's dying and she wanted to take me with her. And I wouldn't do it for her. Wouldn't help her. I spent the night in fucking jail while Cheyenne did something for her that I couldn't.

"Surprise!" Chey tries to sound happy. I'm jealous of her for that. For having it in her to pretend things are okay unlike me who just gets pissed. For doing something for Mom that I should have done, but didn't. And when she wanted it, I wouldn't have been able to do it for her anyway.

"What are you doing here?" I throw at Cheyenne. She flinches and I feel like a fucking prick, but I can't make myself take it back either.

"I would think that's pretty obvious," Chey says. I can tell she wants to say a whole lot more than that, but she's holding off. For Mom.

"If you're going to act like that, Colton, you can turn around and walk right back out of here. This isn't Cheyenne's fault. I wanted a tattoo and I called her. Frankly it's none of your damn business."

Mom's words are like a slap because I want Chey to be my business and Mom always has been.

I step up to them and Chey walks away from the bed. I grab Mom's wrist and look at the swirl of letters.

Colton.

It's simple. Plain black and not very big. It rests on her pulse point. Christ, it had to hurt for her to get a tattoo there.

But she did it. For me. She went out there were she could have gotten sick or anything could have happened. "This was stupid, Mom. Where did you go?"

"Nowhere," Chey answers for her. "I wouldn't do that. I brought someone here."

I can't make myself look at Cheyenne which makes me an even bigger asshole than I already was. I'm wearing the same clothes from yesterday. Sat my ass in jail for a baggie with a little weed while she was taking care of my mom.

I shouldn't be pissed at her for that.

"You shouldn't have done this," I tell Mom. "I . . ." don't want her to die. This somehow means she's really going to fucking die.

"I needed to, Colt. I think it's beautiful. I wanted to do more, but I decided simple was better."

I actually want to fucking cry hearing her speak. She never calls me Colt. Never. But she is now. And she needed my name in her skin.

"Well, it's my name. It has to look badass." The words don't feel nearly as real as I make them sound.

"That's more like it," she says. I lean down and kiss her forehead. She feels clammy.

"I'm going to go. It looks beautiful, Bev." Chey walks across the room.

My eyes dash to Cheyenne, back to Mom and then to Cheyenne again.

"Maggie was about to help me clean up. Why don't you go with Cheyenne?" Mom lies. But I do it. I grab onto that lie because I'm fucking weak.

"Yeah. Okay." I look at the tattoo again. It's red and

irritated, but does look good. My name. To take me with her.

Anger and pain collide inside me so strong I feel like I could erupt right here.

"I'll see you later."

I don't say a word to Cheyenne as we head outside. Her car is two down from mine. I can't believe I didn't notice it.

"Colt. I didn't know what to do. She called and I couldn't get a hold of you. But I'll tell you right now, I don't regret it."

Is it crazy that I'm proud of her for standing up to me at the same time that I'm pissed at her? "Not now. Meet me at home."

Knowing her, she won't go. Maybe I don't want her to. I don't wait around to find out though. I get in the car and drive off.

The second I pull up I hear music blasting from inside. Just what I don't fucking need tonight.

Chey pulls up behind me and slams her door. "You're being a prick, Colt. It's just a tattoo. You have a million of them. She's a grown ass woman if you didn't notice."

"And she's my mom, Chey. Mine. You should have talked to me first."

"I couldn't get a hold of you!" she screams as we stand in the dying grass. "I called you a hundred times and you didn't answer. I didn't—I was—don't be pissed at me when you didn't answer your fucking phone!" She throws her hands in the air as though she's done with me.

And I wouldn't blame her.

"Why are you so mad anyway? Is it because I'm getting too close?"

Christ, but she's not close enough if you ask me and that might make me more mad. "I brought you to meet my mom, Cheyenne. That's as close as anyone's ever been to me."

"Then what the hell is your problem!"

I suddenly can't hold it in anymore. No matter how hard I want to. No matter how much I hate the words or the feeling or sharing them out loud. "What's my problem? I spent the night in fucking jail, Chey. My mom asked me about the tattoo and I was too much a fucking pussy because of shit going on with us to deal with it and I took off. And then—"

My whole body is tense as I remember the woods. Smashing my phone. Crying. When the fuck was the last time I cried?

And realizing I wanted her. I really cared about this girl and then . . . "Yeah. Sorry if I couldn't answer the phone. I was locked up."

And this girl who means way more to me than I ever would have thought, was there for Mom when I couldn't be.

I look at her dark eyes that look sad at my

revelation about jail. Her plump lips, that I can only see because of the porch light behind us. Her caramel skin and remember what her skin feels like under my hands. Under my body.

And what I'd decided before those stupid fucking red and blue lights in my rearview.

That I cared about her.

Looking at her here I know it's more than that. Fuck, how could I have fallen in love with her? With anyone?

"I can't. I have—I gotta go."

A voice in my head is screaming at me the whole time I'm walking away from her. Through the dying grass and opening the front door.

There has to be at least seventy-five people in my house, which is a whole hell of a lot, considering how small it is. I can hardly get through the crowd. The music hurts my ears. People grab and talk to me as I push my way toward the hall.

I don't know what it is, but I remember that night at the party with Chey. When I found her fighting with her ex and how she freaked out and hid behind the shed.

Her panic. The loud music. The people.

"Fuck." I turn around, hoping like hell she didn't follow me inside. I know she's pissed and even though my heart is slamming and I realize now I want nothing more than her with me, I hope she turned around.

Yeah she goes to parties often, but she always panics when she's emotional and I was a big enough asshole to make her pretty emotional.

I see her stumble as she tries to make it through the crowd. Her hands are on her ears and her eyes wide.

Adrenaline shoots through me, fueling me as I shove people out of my way to get to her. Her little body gets squeezed between people. Nothing matters, but her.

"Get the fuck out of my way," I say as I push people. No one can probably hear me, but it makes me feel like I'm doing something.

I get to her and put my arms around her. She might freak out and hit me, but I probably deserve it. I just need to hold her and make everything okay.

"It's okay, baby. I'm sorry. I'm so sorry," I say in her ear. Her arms wrap around me and I let her. Chey buries her head in my chest and I push through the crowd. My room is empty like I knew it would be. That's the one party rule. No one allowed in my room.

I lean against the door, fumbling to lock it and hold her at the same time. "I'm sorry. You're okay, baby," is all I can say over and over and over. It's nothing. Words don't mean shit because I obviously don't treat her right.

Music still beats through the walls. Laughter and

screams from the losers all through the house. I wish I could silence them all for her. Take her wherever she needs to go to come back to me.

"I'm going to lay you down, okay? Let's lay down."

I know she hates to be babied and hates to be seen like this. I hate that she gets like this, but . . . I almost feel like someone special when I help her through it.

With one of my hands I shove the comforter back. I lay her down, pull off her shoes, kick out of mine, and crawl in behind her. I don't know if it's the right thing to do or not, but I pull the blanket over our heads. Trying to give us our own world where I don't get pissed at stupid things, she doesn't have anything to panic over and our moms are okay.

She starts to move and I'm suddenly fucking panicked she's going to pull away from me, but she turns over and slips an arm around me. I pull her close. Wishing she could climb inside me or me her. Anything to keep her safe and be as close as we can.

"I'm here. I have you. Just breathe."

I feel and hear her take deep breaths. Her body's not shaking as bad as it was, but I tighten my hold on her, just to let her know I'm here and won't let go.

"I hate this," she finally says, her voice so soft I can hardly hear her. "I hate being weak."

"You're not weak. You're so fucking strong,

Cheyenne." And not because of this. Because she just is. "You deal with shit so much better than I do."

"I have panic attacks." The words make her shake even harder again.

I know she needs to work through this and I know we need to talk, but right now, I just want her better. I want to ease the tension in her body and make it all go away for her.

"Shh. Not now. It'll be there to talk about later."

"I'm tired . . . so tired. I didn't sleep last night."

Guilt rips through me. Was she worried about me? Christ, it makes me feel like more of a prick. Too proud to use my one call. "Sleep. I got you."

"I'm sorry," she whispers.

"Don't be sorry. It's not you. Shh. We'll talk later." I kiss her head and run my hand up and down her back. "I love you," falls from her sleepy lips. They're so quiet, so mumbled I'm not sure if I heard her right.

Still, the words rock through me. Don't make me want to run. They don't even scare me. I don't know what the hell I did to deserve them or even if I do, but I'm not going to walk away from them.

"You, too." I don't know if she hears me because she doesn't reply. I'm selfish enough I mean them, though. Which is crazy in itself. I fell for this girl and her for me.

Somehow, my bed and the blanket works. We're

in our own world. The music or anyone outside the room doesn't matter. Just us.

I hold her while she sleeps. I don't know how in the fuck we got here, but somehow this game is more real than anything else.

And I want it.

I fucking want it.

CHAPTER TWENTY-SEVEN

CHEYENNE

Lips ghost across my skin. It's dark—I think. I know there's a blanket over me. A hard body against me and that uniquely Colt scent.

Colt.

The evening comes back to me. Our fight, my panic attack. Him taking care of me. Again.

My muscles go rigid. I'm half mad at him for how he acted and half mad at myself for needing him. I shouldn't need him or anyone . . . though is it okay to lean? I don't know, especially since I don't know how he feels.

Little flashes blip through my mind. Did I tell him I love him? I think I did. Or maybe I just said the words in my head. My pulse starts going crazy.

"Tiny Dancer . . ." Colt whispers in my ear. I smile at the name. His hand finds its way under my shirt as he brushes his thumb back and forth on my belly.

Smile or not, I don't reply, hoping he'll think I'm still asleep. Maybe I didn't say them. We need to talk.

I know it, but there's so much going on in my head—in our lives, that I don't even know where to start. All I know is I have questions for him, but I'm not sure I'm ready to answer any.

"Is this what guys talk about when their girl pretends to sleep because she's not in the mood for sex? I promise, you'll enjoy yourself."

This makes me chuckle, which I realize was his point. Who is this man and how do I know him so well? When did it happen and how can someone be so much more than you ever thought they could be?

We're both quiet for a minute. I hear the wheels turning in his head, matching the beat to the ones in mine. We have his mom to discuss, and jail, freak outs, and my possible half-asleep confession. Why the hell can't it be easy?

"Sounds like the party died down," I say, thinking it's the safest thing to talk about. There's no music pounding through the walls anymore.

"I'm an asshole," is Colt's reply. And he is . . . but he isn't at the same time. His hand is still under my shirt, his lips press against my neck. I think it's easier this way—our darkness like he said. Easier to hide and easier for us to come clean in these shadows too.

"You are . . . but I understand. You were just protecting your mom."

"No." Colt rolls to his back. I follow, lying on my

side with my arm around him. We're fully dressed, except for our shoes. "I was being an asshole to her. I was protecting myself. It shouldn't have been a big deal to get her a fucking tattoo."

"Why—"

"—Because it's final." His hand tightens, nails biting into my skin. I can't help but wonder if that means I do something for him too. If somehow I help him the way he helps me.

"I'm sorry." Words are so ridiculous sometimes. They don't really mean anything, but they're all I have. "You have to know she did it because she loves you though. And no matter what, she knows how much you love her."

More silence. His grip has loosened slightly, his thumb moving again. With each swipe I feel closer to him, which I know makes no sense, but it's true.

"I need to make it up to her . . . My head was just all fucked up. We had this crazy talk and I was all over the place. Then I got pulled over. Got searched. Went to jail. So you were taking care of her while I was locked up. I felt like shit and I took it out on you."

His words knock me for a loop. Yes, Colt is always honest. He doesn't hold back, but usually that's when he's being a jerk, not opening up. I never expected to hear these words from him. Don't know what to think about them. All I do know is they make my heart expand. They're the blood pumping life into that vital organ because somehow I know it's because it's me. He feels comfortable baring himself to me.

"You're going through a lot."

"Which is a bullshit excuse. I don't like excuses. What did I tell you that first night? You said your mom left you and I said 'so.' It is what it is and I should know that." His voice sounds so resolved. It's tense, but also like he's made his decision and now he knows there's nothing to do, but go with it.

I'm jealous of him for that. I know how I feel about him, but stressing trying to figure out if I said it out loud or if he heard me. I can't sleep because of the nightmares. I know Mom's gone, but I can't deal with it.

"Don't let this go to your head, but you're stronger than you think."

"So are you, Tiny Dancer." Colt swipes his hand and pushes the blanket from off us. "It's fucking hot under there."

I think I got off easy with the change of subject, but just as quickly as the blanket was gone, he's pulling me over so I'm lying on him. "What happened to you?" He's looking up at me, and me down at Colt. I only see faint shadows of him from the light shining through his window.

Colt pushes a piece of hair behind my ear. It's such a boyfriend thing to do. Not an

I'm-sleeping-with-you-for-fun thing. It both scares and excites me. Maybe he feels the same . . .

Fear wins out. "This guy got all mad at me and pissed me off."

"Be real with me."

He's almost more serious than I've ever seen him. It takes my breath away.

"I thought this was a game," I remind him.

"Not anymore and you know it. Everything else in my life is all fucked up. This is the only thing that's real."

I gasp. It's what I want to hear. What I need to hear. What I feel in each of my scarred heartbeats.

"I'm tired of running." Colt fingers my hair. "I want one thing that's not broken . . . that's not fucked up or dying. Mom's life has always been broken. She had a drug addicted mom and lived in the system. My old man was a prick and a druggie. This is the only thing that's real. Don't run from me, Tiny Dancer."

Each of his words pump up my heart—so big and full I think it might explode. Or maybe it's just the right pressure.

"I'm not going anywhere," I tell him. I think the corners of his mouth tilt up in the dimpled-sexy smile. "I'm more real with you than I've ever been with anyone in my life."

And it's true. How long was I with Gregory and he didn't know about the panic? Aunt Lily knew, but I always played it off as best I could. Even with the doctors.

Only Colt's seen me at my worst and he's still here. Wanting more of the darkness from my past. Looking at his shadowed outline below me, I realize I want to give it to him. That I might be willing to admit, for the first time, I need someone to help me into the light.

I lay my head on his chest. Feel his heart beat against my cheek. I wish we were as physically bare as we are emotionally.

One of Colt's hands slides under my shirt, teasing the sensitive skin at the small of my back, while the other runs through my hair. I'm struck again at how close we are. I wonder if he realizes how much he's giving me right now.

"My mom was the youngest . . . spoiled and rebellious. She got into a lot of trouble and my grandparents always let her slide. She kept it up and according to my aunt, ran away with a boyfriend when she was eighteen. She hadn't finished high school yet. Of course she got pregnant with me and it didn't last. She went back home, but the urge to party was too much so she left again—taking me with her.

"I don't really remember my grandparents. When they died in a car accident, I guess she got worse. Aunt Lily says they didn't know where we were half the time and then Mom would show up with me.

She'd leave me with them for a few days, come back and take me away again."

I hate the way the story sounds. The way it paints her. I'm not sure if that's good or not. "She was funny though. She used to make me laugh all the time."

Colt's so silent, if it weren't for his hands forever moving I would think he fell asleep. I'm thankful for the quiet. I don't know if I would keep going if he interrupted me.

"Anyway, long story short. She still liked to party and she'd bring me with her. At one of the parties, she took off—probably with a guy or something. She told me to stay in the room."

I burrow close to him, hoping his heart against my cheek will pump strength into me.

"It was dark . . . so dark, and this man and woman came in. They were laughing and kissing. The music was loud in the house. I tried to hide, but they turned the light on and saw me. They laughed and I ran."

I stiffen, the familiar thud of panic pulsating through me.

"I got you." Colt squeezes me. I've never felt as close to another human being as I do in this moment.

"It was crowed . . . so crowded and loud. I couldn't hear anything over the music. All I wanted was my mom. I pushed through the people. They spilled beer on me and tripped over me, but I couldn't find her. She was lost."

I take a couple deep breaths.

"I stumbled into the backyard and finally, finally I could hear. The music was in the background, but I still couldn't find her. I started to cry. That's when the guy found me . . . he was big, with a big scruffy beard, I'll never forget it."

Colt cursed. I've never heard his voice so tight. "Did he hurt you?" I feel him swallow hard, his stomach against my chest.

A few tears spring free. "Almost." I whisper.

I'll help you find your mama.

"He told me he'd help me find her. At first he grabbed me and I was scared, but then he said he knew where she was and I went with him. I didn't know. I swear to God, I didn't know, Colt."

I'm crying harder now. The tears flow freely, wetting his shirt. Colt's hands tighten around me. He shushes me and kisses the top of my head.

"You don't have to say anymore, baby. Christ, I'm sorry. So fucking sorry I asked."

I shake my head because now I need to get it out. I need to say it for the first time in my life.

"We were in an old, rundown neighborhood. The house next door was empty and he brought me to it. I remember my heart pounding so hard. I don't think it ever beat that hard, but all I wanted was my mom. I wanted to find her and go home where we could laugh and be normal.

"As soon as the door closed behind me he shoved me into a wall. I hit my head and fell. I remember freezing. I knew I should get up and do something. Run, but I couldn't make myself do it.

"He bent down."

Please. Please, stop.

"His beard scratched my face. His breath made me want to puke."

Colt's so still I don't know if he's even still breathing. He's holding me so tight, it hurts, but I need it too.

"How old were you?"

"Seven."

He curses again.

"His hands were at my pants, Colt. They were unbuttoned and unzipped. I tried to kick him and he hit me. He went for my pants again."

God this is hard. So, so hard. "That's how close I was, to . . . But someone came in. It sidetracked him. I finally made myself run. I ran all the way home in the middle of the night and she was there. She'd forgotten about me and left me. How could she forget me?"

Colt sits up, holding me in his lap. My arms go around his neck and I cry. I cry for that little girl who learned that night never to count on anyone. For the one who still didn't want my mom to leave me when she brought me to Aunt Lily's. The one who felt abandoned. Who never let Lily in. Or

Gregory. Who made the panic seem like less to the doctors because I thought if I somehow made myself perfect, it would mean the people I loved wouldn't leave me.

Who asked Colt to be my fake boyfriend just to prove to Gregory I didn't need him.

I cry for the person I am now. Who doesn't know if I should hate my mom for leaving me. If she really did abandon me or if I wanted her to have or not.

"You don't have to do it on your own. Let me take some of the weight, baby."

But he has so much already. "You have your own problems."

"We'll share each other's."

My hand tightens in his hair and I keep crying. Colt doesn't pull away. Doesn't rush me. Just holds me like he's done so many times before.

Finally after what feels like an eternity, my tears stop.

It must be really early morning because the sun is beginning to rise, little flecks of light started to break through the blinds on his window.

I look at Colt. His eyes look red. From lack of sleep or maybe from something else. I don't know. His hand cups my cheek. "You okay?" he finally asks. We're close. So close as I sit on his lap.

"Yeah . . . thank you."

"I'm fucking good at this boyfriend shit. Who would have thought?" Boyfriend. I like the sound of that. I give him a small smile because it's all I can muster. I appreciate the attempt though.

I suddenly need him more than my next breath. To feel him in a way I've never felt anyone else. Yes, we've done this before. I've done it before. But this will be different.

"Please . . ." I try to climb closer to him. Inside him. "I need you."

"Chey . . ."

"No. Don't do that. It's okay. Nothing's changed."

We both know that's a lie. Everything's changed, but not in the way he's thinking.

"I love you," I say again, this time completely awake and in control of my words.

He presses his lips gently to mine. "You too . . ."

I gasp a little, shocked that he said it. No he didn't use the word love, but it's close enough.

"I told you earlier too." He seems to read my mind.

"I didn't hear you."

When he stands up, I whimper thinking he's going to walk away. Colt crooks his finger at me. "Come here, Tiny Dancer."

My heart raps frantically against my chest. Heat floods my body. I look at him.

And stand.

CHAPTER TWENTY-EIGHT

COLT

I'm being a prick again, but I can't seem to stop myself. She just told me about a man putting his hands on her and here I am about to strip her bare and do the same thing. I should just hold her at a time like this, but Christ, I want her and she wants me too.

That has to make it okay.

"I'll never let anyone hurt you," I tell her, hoping that makes it okay.

"I know."

My hands slip to her waist. I push her shirt up and then pull it over her head. Her yellow bra contrasts against her dark skin. It's so sexy.

I suddenly feel like a jerk because she's slept in these clothes all night. I should have undressed her earlier. It had to have been uncomfortable.

Leaning forward, I tease her lips open with my tongue. I need to taste her. Feel her as she takes a dip and tastes me too. It's so fucking crazy being here with her like this. We've had sex before, but this is

229

different, which makes me feel like a pussy for thinking it, but I don't care.

This girl is mine. I've had quite a few girls before, but none of them were mine. I didn't want them a part of me, to keep them, and with her I want nothing more than to keep her safe and keep her with me all the time.

Our mouths continue to lick and suck and tease at each other as I work the clasps on her bra. I swear she fucking purrs against my mouth as it falls to the floor.

I pull away because there's no way I can't not look at her right now. At her slender body, all dark and toned. "You're so sexy."

This gets a smirk out of her. Her hands are on me now, pushing my shirt off. I'm so hard for her. I'm about to make love to this girl. Damn that sounds stupid thinking of it that way, but it's true.

And I can't wait anymore.

I wrestle with her pants, pushing them down. Her panties match her bra in color and the fact that I want them off her and on the floor.

Mine come next. We're both grabbing at them and laughing. Fucking laughing because we're in such a hurry to have each other. It's never been like this—with her or anyone else.

I grab a condom from the drawer. Chey's lips come down hard on mine. We're fucking frantic and needy and urgent. I pick her up before covering her body with mine on the bed. I kiss her again. Her hands pull at my hair.

"Colt . . . hurry up."

We're laughing again. I never laugh like I do with her. Hours ago I was pissed and fresh from jail and being a prick to my mom, but now I'm here with her . . .

Happy.

I'm fucking happy.

"I want to play," I tease her. Flick her nipple with my tongue. One then the other. Her legs wrap around me and I push against her, feeling, not going inside.

Chey moans. Arches toward me and I know if I don't fill her, I'm going to go insane.

I rip the package open with my teeth. My forearms rest on the bed, one on each side of her head.

Her dark eyes look up at me, spotlighted with the rising sun from outside.

My eyes don't leave hers as I push inside. Who the hell cares how it sounds because this feels different too. She clutches my back and I take her lips. We're moving together and it feels so good I could explode right now.

Our bodies are slick with sweat and I love how that feels too.

I keep going. Harder. Faster. For her. For me. Because I want to keep this up. I want to keep this feeling. Of her. Of being happy.

This isn't a fucking game anymore. No charades here. I don't know exactly what to call it, but whatever it is, it's ours. I'm going to latch onto it. And never let go.

Chey's half on top of me, my hand in her hair, her breath on my chest. She's not asleep, though we've laid here about thirty minutes, neither of us talking.

We have so much shit to deal with: my mom, my upcoming court date, her panic. It's all there, but not right now because in this room, it's like there's no one but us.

I sit up, not wanting to leave the bed, but I have to piss and we have a lot of shit to do. I'm on the edge of the bed, my white comforter around her. "No," Chey says reaching for me.

"I need to get up."

"You need to stay in this bed because if you get up, I have to get up, and I'm exhausted." It's crazy, but I hear the smile in her voice.

I turn to her. "I know I wore you out, but—" My words are cut off with her playful shove. Laughing, I try to get out of the bed, but then she's sitting up, naked behind me. One of her arms is wrapped around my shoulder and the other, under my other arm. She latches her hands together.

"You're not going anywhere."

"Or I'll just take you with me," I smirk. She laughs

and I'm laughing again. I look to the side so I can see her had peeking over my shoulder. "I know I'm hard to resist."

That earns me an eye roll.

The words are out of place here, but they come out anyway. "I want to make it up to Mom. Do something for her today. You wanna go?"

Another smile. It goes straight to my dick, making me hard. Chey rests her chin on my shoulder. "I wouldn't let you go without me."

"About what you told me earlier . . ."

"I know. I need to deal with it."

"I'll help you." Who knows if I even can, but I want her to know I'll be there.

"I know," she answers again. "Now come on. Let's go see your mom."

"I still can't believe you're tatted. That's badass." I wink at Mom. We're sitting on a blanket outside the apartment complex. I don't know if it was smart to bring her out here, but she wanted some fresh air and fuck, if there's one thing you should be able to have, it's air.

We had a picnic, though she didn't each much. Hell, I don't really know if she ate anything, but she's smiling and keeps looking up at the sun or over at me and Chey.

"I'm a badass Mom. What can I say?"

Cheyenne, Mom and I all laugh. I look at her. Her

blue eyes that match mine, but with those purple circles around them. But her smile. It's so big, so bright, so fucking happy.

Christ, I'm going to miss her. She's all I've ever had.

"Don't," she whispers, somehow reading my thoughts. Chey reaches over and squeezes my hand. I try to smile. I'm not sure how real it looks, but I manage it.

Clouds are starting to ease in and I know we don't have much more time. I'm surprised we even got this much warmth and sunshine today.

"Did it hurt?" I ask her.

"Yes! Didn't yours?"

"Pfft. No."

"She did awesome though. She didn't flinch once," Cheyenne adds. I'm jealous she had that with Mom, but glad too. Glad if anyone had to be there for her besides me that it was my girl.

"That's because it was my baby's name. How can I flinch doing one of the most beautiful things I've ever done?"

Her words hit me in the chest. It's like a hammer to my heart, beating it, but somehow it won't break either. It's bruised. Bruised as hell, but it won't shatter over something she did for me.

I reach over and take her hand. I have Chey's on one side and Mom's on the other. And I think . . . I wonder if maybe this—*this* moment is one of the most beautiful for me. I never really cared about beauty before. Not unless I was looking at a girl to hook up with and that's a different kind of beauty. I wonder if I'll look for it now. In other places.

"I'm sorry. About yesterday." I didn't plan to bring it up, but I think needs to be said. "I was a jerk, but I'm glad you did it. I'm honored you did it."

Her eyes swim with tears. "I know, baby boy. I know." Then she looks over at Chey. "Let's talk about you. I want to know everything I can about the girl who stole Colton's heart."

When Chey looks at me, I see she has tears in her eyes too. I nod my head at her and she starts to talk. I watch and listen to them as Chey tells Mom about her dancing. How much she loves it. How it gave her something to focus on when her mom left. She tells her about her mom too. Not all the details, but how things hadn't been perfect and how she recently found out she passed away.

They talk about school and how Cheyenne loves English, but she's thinking about doing something to help kids. Psychology or something. I can't believe I didn't know that. That I didn't take the time to ask. There are so many things I've been doing wrong—for years and as I watch them, my girl and my dying mom, I know I need to fix it. Make it better.

They get on the subject of pictures. It's getting cooler outside and I see Mom shiver.

"Why don't we go inside and look at some? Show Chey I've always been as gorgeous as I am now."

They agree and I have to lift Mom to put her in the chair. I feel her bones through her skin, and that robe she still wears.

Another hammer. More shots, hitting the target they aim for.

We spend an hour going through old pictures. Cheyenne laughs and cries. Mom does too. I almost feel on the outside looking in, but it's okay. I'm a part of it too. She's always worked so hard. She didn't have a lot of friends. Her spare time was spent with me until I was too much of an asshole son and was out all the time. Still, me or work. That's all she ever cared about.

It's fun watching her with Chey. Like she has a friend, or a daughter. I wonder if she sees it that way. I'm glad I gave it to her.

Mom finally admits she's getting tired. She hugs Chey goodbye before I help her to her room. She's in bed and I lean over to kiss her forehead, but she stops me.

"Thank you." Her hand cups my cheek and tears spill down her face. "This day has been perfect, Colton. Just like you, it will always be a part of me."

I shake my head. My eyes ache as I try to fight

back tears. I can't do this. We can't do this now. It's not time. I'm not ready.

"We'll have more of them." I tell her, but I can't look her in the eyes when I say it. "I promise."

"I know." She leans her forehead against mine and we just sit there. I close my eyes because I'm fucking weak and I can't handle seeing her. To see if she doesn't believe we'll have more days like this and wishing I gave her some earlier.

I know she wants to say more. I feel it in the way her hand touches my cheek, but she doesn't. All she says is, "Now go spend the day with that girl of yours. She's something special."

I nod. Stay here a few seconds longer before I pull away. "Yeah . . . she is. I'm lucky to have her."

"She's just as lucky to have you."

I hope so. I really fucking do.

CHAPTER TWENTY-NINE

CHEYENNE

Colt doesn't feel like doing anything after we see his mom. Which I understand. I can't imagine going through what he is and wish there was something I could do for him. I hate feeling helpless. I know it's something I share with him. I think we've both felt like that too often. It's probably one of the things that drew us together.

We stay at his house again. It's wild and crazy as ever. I wonder if Adrian does anything but party.

"How do you handle the partying all the time?" I ask as we lay in bed the next day.

Colt shrugs. "Because I was always partying with him?"

"Oh." His reply makes happiness shoot through me. He's with me instead of partying. "I'm more fun, aren't I?" I tease.

Colt laughs. I love the sound.

"You're fucking cocky is what you are."

"You have the worst mouth."

"I thought we decided women like my mouth. You like my mouth, don't you?"

He starts to use it on me and I can't help but shiver. He definitely knows how to use it.

"You're always distracting me." I let my eyes close and just feel.

"You like that too."

And he's right. I do. I also like this playful side of him. Love that I'm the one who gets to see it.

"Stop talking." My hand slides through his hair.

"Done," he says. Like always Colt makes good on his word.

"Have you done this before?" I ask Colt as he climbs the grassy hill. A few people are already sitting on the ground, different colored blankets under them or some with chairs. There are a few trees, but not a lot. Probably why they do this in the Fall so it's not too hot. Tonight will be chilly though. I'm looking forward to that.

"What?" he replies. I almost forgot I asked him a question.

"The concerts in the park. Have you come to them before?" They're sponsored by the college. Indie type bands play at them. We don't even know what kind of music to expect, but felt like getting out of the house. Like doing something normal.

Colt rolls his eyes at me. "Yeah. All the fucking time. I help organize it."

I shake my head and laugh at him. "You're right.

What could I have been thinking? It would require you to actually want to do something normal or happy."

He does something that surprises me then. Colt tackles me. He's careful and I go down easily because . . . well because I don't mind being taken down by him.

He sits on my stomach, straddling me. He's able to hold both my hands in one of this and I can't get away. "How's this? Is this normal and happy? Is this what I'm supposed to do? Tickle you and be all fucking sappy in public?"

His voice is light. A smile tilts his mouth.

"No. You're not doing it right," I tell him.

He cocks his head. "I'm not? Fuck."

"You're supposed to kiss me."

Without a word he leans forward and does just what I said. Our tongues dance together, around each other the way he calls me Tiny Dancer. All too soon he's pulling away.

"She's good at that, isn't she?" At the sound of Gregory's voice, I tense.

Colt doesn't though. He's off me and on his feet in two seconds.

"What the fuck did you just say?" Colt hisses.

I scramble to my feet. What did I ever see in Gregory? "Don't." I grab onto Colt's arms.

"I said she's good at that, though I'm pretty sure

you heard me." Red is by his side. I'm surprised he doesn't have a friend with him. He's such a coward.

"Don't say a word about her again. Talk shit about me all you want. You bring her into it and I'm going to have to beat your ass. Again. How many times will that make?" Colt starts holding up, one, two, three, four, five fingers until he's holding both hands up.

"Are we really going to do this again?" Colt asks. "I'm down if you are, but you have your girl with you and I'd hate for her to have to clean you up again. Why don't you go do what you came here to do. Talk shit about me to your friends later and pretend you're man enough to matter to me. If you couldn't tell, I'm trying to kiss my girl."

I know Colt. He really will fight if Gregory tries anything. I tighten my grip on his hand. Gregory's face is bright red. He's pissed and embarrassed. I can't believe I was with him so long. That I was so much like him.

"This isn't over," Gregory says before walking away. It's hard not to laugh. It's such a "B" movie thing to say.

"I really fucking hate him." The tension in Colt finally releases.

"I'm sorry. I just want to have a good day."

He sighs, which doesn't sound very good, but says, "We will. We're normal and happy, remember?"

I smile before we finish trekking up the hill, find a spot and lay our blanket down.

The music starts not long after. A guy with a guitar who sounds a little like Bobby Long, one of the only people I really listen to. This guy isn't as good.

I sit between Colt's legs and he has his arms around me. I feel his heart against my back and wonder if mine matches his rhythm.

When it starts to get cold, he pulls the blanket around us. Gregory's forgotten. Everything else can wait. We just sit back and listen. I'm not even sure if he likes this kind of music, but he's here and that means something to me.

"You owe me for this," he whispers in my ear before nipping it with his teeth.

"How did I know you'd say something like that?"

He chuckles and keeps holding me. I'm glad it's cold, but even if it was a hundred degrees I would still love to have him wrapped around me.

When it's over we hold hands as we walk back to the car. I'm not sure how many more days we'll have like this—if it was a fluke because he just needed a break or if we'll try to make this our new normal. All I know is I loved it. I love everything I do with him.

"We just went on a fucking date, Tiny Dancer," Colt teases when we get to the car.

"I was just thinking that."

He smirks. "It wasn't so bad. Mom will be proud."

I return his smile before hugging him. What is it about this boy that makes me come undone? That makes me need to touch him and talk to him and just be with him?

"Did you only go out with me to make your mom happy?" I laugh.

Colt shakes his head. "Are you trying to pull compliments out of me?"

I playfully push him before getting in the car. He's right behind me, tossing the blanket into the backseat and then climbing into the passenger side.

I hardly have the car started when my phone rings. It's Bev's number. Colt doesn't have a new phone so maybe she's just calling to say hi. "Hello." I listen. Tears automatically pool in my eyes. My heart breaks. "Okay . . . I understand."

I hang up the phone and look at Colt. "That was Maggie." I grab his hand and he tenses. "She's not doing well . . . They're calling in hospice. They think it's time."

That quickly, our normal . . . our happy, is over.

CHAPTER THIRTY

COLT

I feel like I'm choking on my own tongue the whole way there. Like it's swelling, filling my mouth, throat, suffocating me, but I still can't make myself open my mouth and say a word. My mind is blank the whole time except for the same words going over and over through my head.

It's time, it's time, it's time.

Such simple fucking words, but they mean everything's changing. That I'll have to keep going on, but she'll soon be dead. Fucking gone. No huge beating heart, no smile. Nothing but skin, bones and my name on her wrist, until eventually she won't even be that anymore.

My grip tightens on the door and the center console as my dancer drives me home. To sit with my mom. While she dies.

I almost gag. Something wants to come up my throat but I fight it down. I can't lose it. Can't. Not yet. Not before I see her.

We get out of the car and Cheyenne takes my hand. She doesn't ask me if I'm okay. What a stupid fucking question that is. I hate it when people ask that when they know the answer. Instead she asks, "Are you sure you want me to stay?"

I pull her to me, loving her for asking and still needing her here because there's no way I can do this alone.

"Stay." Is all I say because it's all I can manage. She nods, understanding. Always understanding no matter how big a prick I've been.

My hands fucking shake as we walk inside. I lace my fingers through hers, needing the grounding only this girl gives me.

"Oh, Colton," Maggie pulls me into her arms, but I don't hug her back. Don't have it in me to do anything.

I don't get it. The day before yesterday, she was fine. Laughing and talking and sitting in the sunshine.

"What happened?" I manage to ask.

Maggie pulls away. "Yesterday she slept most of the day. Was vomiting."

"Why didn't you call me?" I ask.

"She asked me not to. Said she was just tired. It's her right, Colton."

"I'm her son." I push around Maggie. "I have a right."

"Another hospice nurse came in this morning . . . They prescribed a lot more morphine. It will help with the pain."

Help kill her, she means.

"She didn't want to take any until you got here. She's still sleeping a lot but—"

I don't hear anything else because I'm down the hall. To her room. She's in fucking pain because she wanted to wait for me.

Her head is turned, her eyes on the door as soon as I step inside.

"Colton," she hardly whispers out. My feet plant to the floor. I can't move. How the hell can she look so much worse in two days? How can it happen like this? She's hooked up to the IV. I've seen her on it at home before, but this is different.

My pulse pounds in my ears. My chest aches. This is Mom. The one who's always been there. The one who wanted nothing but for me to be happy. To make something of myself. To be more than her and more than my dad and she's fucking dying.

Her arm stretches out, her hand open to me.

Fucking move, Colt!

I feel Chey's hand on my shoulder, urging me on. One foot in front of the other I go to her.

"Hey, Mom." My voice breaks and I hate myself for it. Hate that I can't be stronger when she needs me.

"Hi." Her lips are cracked they're so dry, but she manages to stretch them into a smile anyway.

"I love you." I'm pissed those are the words that come out of my mouth. I love her and want her to know but that's what you say before goodbye. I'm not ready for goodbye yet.

She doesn't answer right away. Just grabs my hand and tries to squeeze. "I'm tired."

"Are you in pain?" What a screwed up question. Of course she's in pain. I'm in pain just looking at her.

Mom nods her head.

"Chey. Get Maggie. Tell her she needs the meds."

I keep holding her hand as I sit in the chair. Neither of us speak. Her breaths are shallow, loud.

It's not Maggie, but another nurse who comes into the room and adds medicine to the IV. Chey's hands touch my shoulders again. I don't look at any of them. Don't talk to anyone. Do nothing but watch her.

CHAPTER THIRTY-ONE

CHEYENNE

Colt's mom's been asleep for three hours. He hasn't spoken a word the whole time. I'm sitting in a chair beside him. He's holding her hand, his head in his arms that are resting on her bed. Sometimes I touch him. I want him to know I'm here. I'll always be here. I alternate between rubbing his back and touching his leg and pulling back to give him space. Still I don't leave the chair. As long as he's by her side I'll be by his.

Longer even.

My heart aches for him—breaks for him and for her. For everyone because this world will be a little more lonely without her in it.

I've only known her a short amount of time and I know that.

His stomach growls, but I don't ask if he wants food. I know he'll say no.

I look at Colt. Look at Bev and flash to Mom telling me goodbye. Flash to what her bones must have looked like in those woods. Alone. I'm glad Bev won't have to go alone like that.

Glad Colt and I won't be left by ourselves either.

He sits up enough to rub a hand through his hair. It's as messy as I've ever seen it. His leg bounces up and down. But he hasn't shed a tear.

For the first time, he turns and looks at me. The pain in his eyes rips through my chest and makes tears spring to my eyes. I'm not as strong as he is.

"Don't cry," he whispers. "Not yet. You didn't cry for yourself for so long. If you do it now, make it for her, not me."

I nod. He leans away from the bed enough to run a hand down the side of my face. To push my hair behind my ear.

The smile he gives me is worse than weeping. It's broken. Pained.

And just that quickly his hand is gone and his head is turned and he's leaning on the bed again. Holding her hand and watching her breathe. The breaths that I begin to count the second between.

Maggie's in and out. The hospice nurse too. Colt doesn't talk to them. They speak to me, but mostly I think they want to leave us alone with her while we wait for her to go.

CHAPTER THIRTY-TWO

COLT

Mom's eyes flutter open for the first time in hours. Five to be exact. They dart around the room, fear peering out of them.

"What is it? What's wrong? Do you need the nurse?"

"I'm late for work!" she says and tries to get up.

Work? She hasn't worked in a year. "Mom . . . you don't work. You're . . ." I can't manage to say it. "Do you need the nurse?"

"I don't want to get fired. I need the money. My son . . ." She looks scared to death. Pulls her hand away from me.

My heart is racing. My body numb. Does she not know who I am? "It's me. I'm your son. You don't have to work. You just need to rest."

"Colton?" her voice cracks, confusion still splintering through.

"Yeah. Yeah it's me." It's me. I have to tell her who I am. I want to scream. To throw up. To wake up from this shitty ass nightmare and find out everything's okay.

"Colton . . ." she says again, this time with recognition. The nurse comes into the room again, fills a syringe and shoots more pain medicine into her.

One, two, three.

Her eyes flutter.

Four, five, six.

She's asleep again.

I fall into the chair.

I've already lost her.

CHAPTER THIRTY-THREE

CHEYENNE

Colt's said a few words, but nothing major. I've held him and given him space. Maggie's brought food we haven't touched. The only time we leave is to go to the restroom.

It's four hours later when her eyes finally open again. How many hours have we been here? I hold my breath. I think my heart stops too.

Please let her be okay. Let her know who he is. Let him be able to say goodbye.

"I . . . wish . . . you . . . didn't . . . have . . . to . . . look . . . so . . . sad . . ." she says, weakly smiling.

I feel the tension leak out of Colt's body.

"Mom. Hey. How do you feel?"

"Happy to see you," she replies.

I know I shouldn't. That I should be strong, but I can't fight the tears from falling down my face. Can't hold them back or reel them in.

And it's not all from sadness. I see the way she looks at him and it's beautiful. She loves him the way a mother should love their child. Thoroughly.

Completely. To her, he's the most important person in the world and I'm so very happy they have that.

"Always trying to get on my good side," Colt tries to tease. I love him more for it.

She reaches for his hand. I didn't realize they'd let go. He gives it to her and she squeezes.

"Let me talk to Cheyenne." Her voice is so soft, I can hardly make out her words. Colt looks like he's ready to panic. His eyes wide as he looks from her to me.

"It's okay," she says. "It'll just be a minute."

I cry harder. I need to stop, but I can't make myself do it. I wipe my eyes as Colt stands up. He kisses her cheek. Stands and drops his forehead against mine.

No words are needed. We just lean into each other. "We'll be okay," I whisper.

He nods.

"I love you."

"You too." And then he's gone. I take his chair and have to lean in close so I can hear her.

"You're beautiful together." Her chin trembles, which makes me cry again.

"I love him. He's . . ."

"Frustrating."

I smile. "Yes."

"But he's wonderful too." Her voice sounds so proud in that moment. You wouldn't know she was sick. She's just a mom proud of her son.

"You guys think you fooled me in the beginning," she rasps. "You were only fooling yourself."

I nod because she's right. I'm not surprised she knows. I'm honored she sees it's real now.

"Take care of him."

The words snap me like a twig. "I will." I can hardly get out between my sobs. I squeeze her hand and rest my cheek on it. "I will, I will, I will."

"Take care of you too. And let him. He doesn't realize it, but he's good at taking care of people."

"He is." I say this with as much conviction as she spoke with. "He takes good care of me."

"You have to be able to take care of yourself too. Both you and Colton. It's okay to lean, but you both need to know how strong you are too."

"I—"

"Your mom loved you," Bev cuts me off. I gasp. My tears are running down onto her hand and I feel guilty, but can't make them stop.

"She loved you. It would be impossible not to. She might not always have known how to show it. She might not have always done the right thing, but she loved you. She loved you," she says again.

"Thank you." I say it over and over. Until my throat is raw. Until she knows how much those words mean to me because somehow they have to be real if she says it.

"He loves you," she adds. "And I love you. You're everything I could have hoped for, for him."

I can't stop myself. I stand up and lean down to rest my head on her chest. The tears don't stop. She shushes me. Runs a hand through my hair. It's the same thing Colt does and I wonder how many bruised knees and bad days she soothed for him this way.

Finally, when the tears are gone, I sit up. "Thank you. I love you too."

A quick nod is my reply. "I need Colton." Her voice is laced with pain. Broken and bleeding with it. "I need my boy."

CHAPTER THIRTY-FOUR

COLT

My feet are weighed down, but I somehow manage to make them move. Chey's in the hallway as I close Mom's bedroom door.

I don't know if it's okay or if it's right or if it makes me the weakest son-of-a-bitch on the planet, but I crawl into bed with her, hoping and praying I don't hurt her. All I know is I need her.

I wrap my arm around her. Curl up on my side. I feel small . . . like a kid. How I used to get into bed with her when I'd have a nightmare or the neighbors would scream so loud they scared me.

"My sweet, sweet, boy," she says. I don't know how she managed to make her voice sound clear, stronger. Probably for me. Because she knows I need it.

"Live your life," she finally says. I have to look up to see her because I don't know what she means.

She sighs. Bites her chapped lip. "You can do anything you want, Colton. That's all I've ever wanted you to know. You're better than me. Better than your father. You can have anything. Be anything. Do anything . . . but live your life. If you decide college isn't what you want, don't do it because of me. I want you to find whatever you can that makes you happy and you hold it. You grab onto it with all your might. If I ever pushed you into anything it's because I wanted you to know you're better than selling drugs, going to jail. Nickle and diming it like I've had to do."

Selling drugs. Going to jail.

Does that sound familiar? The things I hated my father for.

Her eyes hold mine intensely. "Just be good . . . be happy. That's all I want for you. And for you to know how one-of-a-kind you are. You are strong, loyal, caring. You make that girl out there smile like she has the world in the palm of her hand." She pauses, breathing hard from the effort of so much talking. Then she whispers, "You gave me the world."

I'm begging myself to say something, but I can't find the words. They're locked inside me. Each time they try and slip through, a door closes on them, blocking them out.

"You gave me the world," she says again. "You're the only thing I've ever done that means something."

"You made me who I am," is what I manage to say.

I hope it's enough. Hope it's right. When I look at her, her face is wet. Tears giving moisture to her lips that are turned up in a smile.

Hours go by. I don't even know how the hell many. They pass as she sleeps and breathes those raspy breaths. She hasn't woken up again for so long. It's the middle of the night now. All I have to do is look at the clock, but I don't have the energy.

Cheyenne's standing by the window, looking out at the darkness. There's only a small light next to mom's bed that's on. A streetlight outside shines against my dancer.

Looking at her, I suddenly need her. To feel her and talk to her. She jumps when the chair squeaks as I stand. Without a word I walk over to her and pull her into my arms. Bury my face in her neck as she clutches at my back.

And somehow . . . I feel better. Still broken and lost and angry, but not so alone too.

I step forward and Cheyenne backwards. She leans against the wall and just lets me hold her. Holds me. "I'm losing her," pushes past my lips, into her neck. "I'm fucking losing her. I don't want to lose anyone else I love. I don't want to lose you." I don't know where the words are suddenly coming from, but I can't make them stop. Can't reel them in. "I'm a prick half the time, but you make me better. You make me happy. I don't want to lose you. I love you. I don't want to lose you."

"I love you too. I'm not going anywhere. We make each other better."

I pull away from her. Put my hands on her hips. Dig my nails in because I need to hold her as tight as I can. And then lean forward and kiss her. It's slow and healing. She moans and I swallow it down. Taste every part of her mouth. Give her mine. Push against her. Pull her to me.

"I want to be someone," I say when I pull away. "I don't know who. I just know I don't want to be the guy who sells weed. The one who busts his phone against a tree when he realizes he fell for a girl. Who goes to jail and takes it out on her because she's there for his mom when he wasn't."

"You are more than that," she tells me.

"I don't know if I am, but I want to be."

"My mom loved me," Cheyenne says, shocking me. "I don't know if she meant to leave me, but she loved me. And I'm not perfect. I don't want to be. I have panic attacks I don't deal with, but I need to. I will."

I kiss her again because she's so fucking strong. In this moment, in the half-dark room while my mom sleeps on the bed next to us, we make our vows to each other. To stop pretending. To grow up. To do what the hell we need to do not be the people who had to play a fucked up game of charades to fall in love.

We're both quiet. Mom's breathing is the only sound in the room. We lean against the wall, holding each other.

"I couldn't do this without you, Tiny Dancer."

"I wouldn't be anywhere else."

I take a couple deep breaths before saying, "I don't want to tell her goodbye." But I have to. I know it. Know she's probably waiting for it.

"I know. I'm sorry."

I kiss her again. "I know."

Daylight has come and passed again. It's the next night. Mom hasn't woken up anymore. Maggie and the hospice nurse come in and out. Give medicine. Sad smiles. Her hand doesn't hold mine anymore, but I try to hold on tight enough for both of us.

I know what I need to do. Every time I open my mouth it won't come out. So I sit here. Watching her die. Watching her suffer. Waiting.

Mom doesn't make any sounds beside the breaths that sound almost painful.

Fucking do it.

I look over at Cheyenne and she's watching me. I try to tell her with my eyes. Let her know that I'm letting her go. She gives me a small nod.

I'm scared to fucking death to do this, but proud too. Proud because I'm setting her free. Letting her be in the sunshine.

I lean forward, my mouth next to her ear. My words are soft, only for her and me.

"I lied to you last time you asked, but I want you to know, I'm happy. You never pushed me unless I needed to be pushed. You gave me everything and I swear to God, I'll make you proud of me. For you . . . and for me too. I love you . . ." My voice breaks. The words unlock the dam that held my tears back and I finally cry. Cry for her. For me. For the whole fucking world who is losing her. "I'm *happy*. I'll be okay. I'll live for me, but for you too. You don't have to worry about me. You can go . . . I have Cheyenne and I fucking love her. Christ. I shouldn't be cursing right now, but I love her. I do. We'll be okay."

I swear her hand tightens on mine. Nothing else moves. Her breathing doesn't change, but I know she hears me. I know she's proud of me. I'm proud of me.

"I love you. I'm okay," I say again.

I lace my fingers with hers and sit on the edge of the bed. I look at Chey and she comes over. She sits behind me, one hand on me and one on Mom.

And we wait.

Seconds.

Minutes.

Half an hour.

Her breathing slows. Softens.

"I'm okay," I say again. Pick up her wrist. Kiss my
name there.

One more breath.

I wait.

And wait.

She doesn't breathe again.

She's gone.

CHAPTER THIRTY-FIVE

CHEYENNE

Colt's silent as the hospice nurse makes a phone call. He's quiet as Maggie cries. I'm scared to death he's going to pull away. That he's going to run. Then I feel like a jerk for even thinking about that. Bev is gone. His mom just died. He just let her go.

"I need to get out of here," he finally says. We leave the apartment and climb into the car. "Can you call Adrian?" He doesn't look at me when he speaks, so he doesn't see my nod.

I pick up my cell, call him. "Can you make sure the house is empty?" I ask. I can understand why Colt would want to make sure no one's there when we get home.

"Already done," Adrian replies.

I don't know how he knew, but it doesn't matter. "Thanks. We appreciate it."

"Take care of my boy," I hear him inhale, shake my head, knowing he's probably sucking weed into his lungs right now.

"I will." I try to put the phone in the cup holder, but it falls between the seats and to the floor. I leave it. It doesn't matter right now. Nothing does except for Colt.

His hand is on my leg the whole way home. I wonder if he needs that connection as much as I do? To know that even though it hurts, there's still someone by my side. And it has to be even worse for him.

As promised, the house looks empty when we get home. Dark. The porch light isn't even on.

Colt lets go of my leg and gets out of the car, but doesn't move. I wish I knew what to do for him. A way to lessen the pain.

Getting out, I walk to the other side of the car.

"I can't believe she's fucking gone." He leans me against my car like he did the wall earlier and holds me.

His grip eases me. How easy would it be for him to run right now? I did when I found out about my mom and our situation was completely different. But he's here. With me. Leaning on me and holding me.

"I love you," I tell him.

"I—"

"—Isn't that fucking sweet?" A male voice comes from behind us. Colt instantly tenses.

"She's got him whipped. At least you were smart enough to keep someone fun on the side, G."

Colt whips around. I feel the anger rolling off of him.

Gregory and three of his friends stand behind us. I smell beer. One of them has a bottle in his hand that he drinks from.

I try to wrap my arms around Colt from behind. We don't need this right now. "Let's just go."

He shakes me off.

"Going to listen to your girl? Don't have a big mouth like you did the other day?" This from Gregory.

"Please fucking hit me, Pretty Boy. I'm begging you. I won't even fight back at first," Colt steps forward. Again I grab his arm and he pulls away.

"Don't do this." I know this isn't even fully about Gregory. He wants to hurt because of his mom. He wants to hurt someone else because of her. I look at Gregory and shout, "You have the worst timing ever. Leave him alone."

"Get in the car, Tiny Dancer." Another step, but I'm right behind him.

"What are you guys even doing here?" I stand next to Colt who again tries to push me behind him.

"He's always showing up where we party. Getting in our business so we thought it was time we returned the favor." My stomach rolls at the sound of Gregory's voice. I can't even believe this is him.

Was he always like this? Something college has done to him?

"Are we just gonna sit around and talk or did you guys come here for a reason?" Colt's voice is tight as he eggs them on. A few steps and he's right in front of Gregory, almost nose to nose with him. "You wanted to teach me a lesson, Pretty Boy? Do it." And then he pushes Gregory.

Gregory stumbles backward.

"What the fuck. Kick his ass, G!" One of his friends yells.

"Don't let that pussy get the best of you again!" Another says.

It all happens so fast from there. Colt pushes me back as Gregory charges, hitting Colt across the middle. They both stumble. Fall backward. I watch him fall in slow motion . . . down . . . down. His head cracks loudly on the curb, Gregory on top of him. I scream, but it's like my body's gone into some sort of shock from disbelief. This cannot be happening.

Colt doesn't move.

"Holy shit!" Gregory scrambles off him. Everything seems normal. Colt looks normal, but it's obvious he's not. Gregory sees it too. "It was an accident. I didn't fucking mean it!" He's pacing.

Hot tears run down my face. There isn't blood.

Why isn't there blood? I'm not sure if that's good or not. My throat hurts, it's raw as I scream and scream. I shove Gregory aside, drop and crawl to Colt. I touch his chest. Stomach. Want to pull his head to my lap, but don't think I should.

My tears hit him, puddling on his shirt. "Get help! Call someone!" I cry. Why isn't he moving? Please let him move.

"I'm getting the fuck out of here!" yells one of them.

Tires squeal at the same time feet hit the ground running.

Please don't die, please don't die, please don't die. Over and over and over the words flow through my head.

I scream, lean over and hold him. "Colt. I'm here. I'm going to get some help." Then I'm fighting when someone tries to pull me away from him.

"Cheyenne!" It's Adrian. "We need to get him to a fucking hospital."

Adrian's voice snaps me out of it. I jerk away as he lifts Colt up. His head flops to the side. "My phone. It's in my car."

"Fuck it. We're driving him there."

I run to Adrian's car. I don't know how I'm even going right now, but I know I have to. Have to do it for Colt.

I rip the door open.

"Get in," Adrian says. He's already laying Colt in the backseat as I try and scoot over. His head is in my lap. It doesn't feel like there's a big injury. I'm not sure if that matters. I keep feeling his pulse, checking his breathing.

It feels like an eternity and at the same time, only a few seconds when we get to the hospital. I hardly remember the ride. I just hold Colt the way he held me in the car not too long ago. Tell him he'll be okay. That I love him. Should we have moved him? What if we hurt him by moving him? Too many thoughts are slamming into me.

Adrian's out of the car and pulling Colt into his arms. We rush through the EMT entrance.

"What are you—Room three!" a nurse yells when she sees Colt in Adrian's arms.

I struggle to see through the tears blurring my vision. One of the doctors grabs Colt. They're laying him on the bed. Two more nurses and a doctor rush in. My heart hurts. I gasp, trying to breathe.

"Please help him." I try to get into the room.

"What happened?" someone asks.

"He was pushed and hit his head on the curb."

One of them curses. "You're going to have to get out of here."

Fear spikes inside me. "No! I'm not leaving him." He wouldn't leave me. I know he wouldn't.

"If you want to help him get out of here, give them

some information and give us space." They rip the curtain closed.

Adrian catches me as I fall. "They're going to fix him. Let them do their job."

"He just lost his mom," I sob. Please let him be okay. Please let him be okay. "I don't want to leave him."

"You're not," he whispers in my ear. "You're making it so they can take care of him. He knows you wouldn't leave him."

My eyes find Adrian. His are bloodshot and I wonder if it's from crying or being high. Whatever the reason, he's somehow calming. And he cares about Colt. He's a good friend.

"Excuse me, miss? We need to get some inform-ation from you," a dark-haired nurse asks.

I nod. After glancing once more at the closed curtain of Colt's room I follow her. Adrian stays with me the whole time — helping with some of the inform-ation on Colt. I don't even know his birthday. How can I not know his birthday?

I tell them what happened. They call the cops, promising to let me know the second they know anything about him.

My legs are shaking so bad it's hard to walk, but I can't make myself sit down either. Adrian watches me the whole time, but doesn't speak. He's always so laid back, but right now, he's uptight. Tense. He looks as panicky as I feel.

The cops come and we still don't know anything about Colt. I tell them what happened. They want to know who pushed who first. I don't want to tell them since it was Colt. It was all a screwed-up accident.

I give them Gregory's full name. I don't know anyone else's.

"Her ex-boyfriend is an asshole. He's a spoiled, rich kid who doesn't like to lose and he lost." Adrian storms out of the room. Guilt knocks the air out of me. Choking me. This is all because of me. Because of the stupid game I made him play.

I finish giving them information and give them my phone number. I'm walking away as I say the last numbers. I wring my hands together as I approach the desk. "I need to check on Colton." I'm almost scared to ask, but I need to know. He has to be okay. Has to.

"Is there any family?" the desk clerk asks. *Me*, I think. I'm family.

"They were asking about parents."

"His mo—" Oh God. How could I have almost forgotten that quickly? Bev is dead. She only died hours ago. I shake my head. "No. His mom just passed away."

She sighs, but I can tell it's because she feels bad.

"Please." I hate begging. Hate it. I'll do anything in this moment. Weakness or strength doesn't matter. Nothing matters but Colt.

Adrian appears out of nowhere, stepping up beside me. I feel like we're a team. The both of us loving the guy in the emergency room. It's crazy because I don't know him well. He's there a lot, smokes a lot of pot. I never would have thought he'd be the kind of guy I'd be friends with, but then I never thought I'd fall in love with Colt either. The both of them are better than Gregory and his friends would ever be.

"Tell us," Adrian says, his voice pained.

She sighs again. "Since you're the one who brought him in, I guess it's okay. Let me get the nurse."

She slips through the door. Again I pace. I've cried so many tears my face is finally dry, but it doesn't change how I feel in the inside. I'm breaking apart in there.

The sliding door opens and it's the doctor who comes out. Adrian slips an arm around me, to steady himself or me, I don't know.

"You're his . . ."

"Fiancé," I lie.

She's a female doctor, with short blond hair. "We ran some scans and there's slight swelling on his brain, and a bleed. It's where the blood is trapped with nowhere to go. When the surgery is done, he'll go into the ICU. We'll give him a couple days, run some more tests in the meantime. We won't know much until then."

I almost fall, but Adrian holds me up.

"He only hit his head!" Which sounds ridiculous, but people fall and hit their head all the time. One minute he was standing there and that quickly, over a stupid fight that has to do with me, he's having surgery and going to the ICU.

"Our heads are very fragile. Sometimes that's all it takes. The truth is, he can wake up and be fine. Have no side effects. You never know with the brain, but . . ."

He also might not. Or have brain damage. I'm sure there are more possibilities than I know about. I don't want to hear them. "Can . . . can I stay with him?"

She nods. "When he's settled in his room. No more than two visitors in the ICU rooms though."

I nod and she goes back into the ER.

"Can I use your phone?" I ask Adrian. He nods. "I don't know Maggie's number. We should call her."

I have no idea how I sound so steady right now. I feel like I'm falling apart.

"Keep my phone. I'll go tell her. Give me the keys to your car too and I'll grab yours."

I give him the keys and Adrian doesn't wait for me to say thank you. He leaves.

My fingers move quickly on the screen. It's late, but Aunt Lily picks up on the second ring. "Hello?"

"Lily. It's Chey. Please come. Colt's hurt. I need you."

I sit at Colt's bed, holding his hand in the same way he held his mom's. It's not right. Not fair, but I'm learning—or maybe I've always known, that life never really is.

Adrian's in the waiting room. He went out so Lily could sit with me. There is a tube in Colt's throat, helping him breathe. There's so many buttons, machines, beeping. Each time an alarm goes off I jump. We don't know when or if he'll wake up.

I can't keep my eyes off him. His hair, his mouth. I want to touch his cheek. Kiss him. Hold him. How can we be here? After Bev we shouldn't be sitting here wondering if Colt will be okay.

I glance back at Lily. She gives me a sad smile, stands up and walks over behind me. Her hands rest on my shoulders and I'm so thankful she's here. I haven't been fair to her. Maybe ever. I never let myself really get close to her after Mom left. Haven't talked to her much since we found out Mom died, but she's here. Here by my side. By Colt's, regardless of how I never really let her in.

I want to deserve her.

"I have nightmares," is the first thing that comes out of my mouth. Lily gives a small gasp behind me, but waits for me to continue. As soon as the words are out I'm glad I'm finally sharing them with her.

"After Mom . . . I've started having nightmares. Really only when I sleep alone. Colt helps. Maybe just to know someone's there. I used to have them right after Mom left . . . died? I don't even know the right word to use. But then, I had them then too." It's a huge weight off my chest. Like I'm bridging the gap between us I always fought to keep there.

"Oh, sweetheart. Why didn't you ever say anything?"

I shrug. "Because I was afraid. I didn't want to be weak. Didn't want to have to depend on anyone. I was scared to count on you because I thought you would leave like she did. Because it had to be me, right? There was no other reason a mom would leave her daughter."

My eyes pool, but I manage to keep the tears from falling.

"It's not you. It was never you, Cheyenne. I hope you know that now."

I nod because I do. "Soon, it was just easy to keep it up. Even when you had me talk to the doctor in the beginning, I didn't tell her. I tried to fight the panic attacks, didn't want the medicine. I guess I was even afraid the stupid pill would leave me."

Her grip tightens on my shoulder. "I used to feel like it was my fault your mom turned out how she did. Maybe I wasn't a good enough sister. I wanted so much to make it right for you and I thought I did. I didn't pay close enough attention."

"No," I whisper, but still can't look at her. "It wasn't your fault. It wasn't anyone's fault." I pause and take a few breaths. "Colt could die . . . . Or have lasting injuries. He just lost his mom and he could lose so much more on top of that. In a second. Because of a stupid fight. We wasted so much time playing games . . . He gave me so much and I never told him."

Lily's hands shake. I know she's crying. But I still keep talking. "I'd like to tell you everything . . . More about growing up and about how I feel . . . If you want to know."

The words aren't as hard as I thought they would be. They actually feel freeing.

"Oh, Cheyenne. I would love nothing more."

"I also want to talk to someone else. A doctor or something. Can you . . . Can you help me set it up?"

"Absolutely."

Finally I turn to look at her, but don't let myself let go of Colt's hand.

"Your mom never asked for help. Not the kind she needed. You're a very strong, brave woman, Cheyenne. I couldn't be more proud of you."

In this moment, I'm pretty proud of me too.

"Thank you." I turn back to Colt. Lay my head on his bed. "You'd be proud of me too. I know it. I can't wait until you wake up so I can tell you."

"How did you and Colt meet?" I ask Adrian. It's been a day and a half. I haven't left the hospital. Adrian's stayed most of the time. Aunt Lily and Maggie have both come and gone. No one tries to make me leave, probably because they know I won't.

"We got into a fight when he fucked around with a girl I was seeing."

I turn and look at Colt's "brother." I'm sure the hospital staff knows we're lying, but they've been okay with it. "Tell me you're kidding."

"Would I lie about something so serious?" He grins, leaned back in the chair. He looks comfortable, but I know he's not. Know he's just as scared as I am.

"You guys are nuts." I shake my head. "What happened?"

"Punched each other a few times. Then I told him he had a nice swing, but he'd screw up his thumb if he kept his fist the way he held it. He told me to fuck off. I asked him if he wanted to smoke a bowl and we were all good after that."

I don't know why I'm surprised. "Guys are so crazy."

Adrian shakes his head. "We're a lot easier than girls. They take everything too serious. Plus, I knew we'd be cool." He taps the side of his forehead.

"That's right. All knowing Adrian."

"You bet your ass. Just like I know he'll be okay. He wouldn't leave you. He's too loyal for that shit. Cares about you too much."

I smile at Adrian and choose to believe him.

Wonder if Adrian needs Colt too. I have a feeling Colt wouldn't want to leave Adrian either.

Another day passes.

"His latest scans look really good. Good brain activity. The bleed is gone. We're going to start decreasing the medication and hope he wakes up. We'll have more answers after that." The doctor smiles at me and I try to return it.

"Thank you."

"You're doing good. Keep doing what you're doing. Hold his hand. Talk to him. I believe he can hear you."

She walks out of the room. I know he can hear me too.

"They've been decreasing your medication, Colt. They say you can wake up any time. I can't wait to see your eyes again. You have to open them for me, okay?"

I try to hold the tears back. I want to sound happy. Strong for him.

"You can even call me princess if you want. Not for long, but I miss fighting with you. Miss that big head and bigger attitude you have."

Leaning forward, I kiss his hand.

"I told Lily I'm going to talk to someone. I think it will help. It's because of you, ya know? That I'm stronger. God, I used to think you were such a jerk. I can't believe I didn't see it. You don't know it, but you're everything, Colt. No one makes me feel the way you do and I need you. Maybe it's not good to need people and maybe that makes me weak. I don't know, but I know I need you. I want you. You push me when I need it and give in when I need that too. Your strength gives me strength and I want to do that for you too.

"My aunt and uncle are taking care of your mom. The funeral home is holding her for you. We don't want to bury her without you. You deserve to be there. But you have to open your eyes, okay. Please open your eyes soon. I love you. I love you. I love you."

The breathing tube is gone. He's able to breathe on his own. They say that's a good sign.

"I brought you a coffee," Adrian sets a drink on the table.

"He looks better." Then he talks to Colt. "You're still not as good looking as me, Colt, but you don't look like shit anymore."

I almost yell at Adrian for saying that, but don't. This is who they are and what they do. We need to treat Colt as we did. That's the best way to get him to come back to us.

*　　*　　*

Darkness is all I see. It's strange, like I know I'm sleeping, but I somehow feel conscious too.

I'm tired. So tired. I try to fight the fact that I'm waking up. I don't get much sleep leaning on Colt's bed.

Something tightens around my hand. I feel myself smile in my half-asleep state. I loved when Colt would squeeze my hand.

It happens again. I don't want to wake up because I don't want to lose it. I love these times Colt meets me in my dreams.

Another squeeze. Weak. Colt holds me harder than that.

My eyes rip open and I look at Colt. His flutter. Open. Close. Open again.

My heart jumps. Leaps. Explodes. Does everything else it can do.

I push the button for the nurse.

"Colt? Can you see me? It's Chey. I'm here."

He studies me, his blue eyes so intense they entrance me. I see familiarity in them.

He opens his mouth, but nothing comes out.

Tears fall down my face. He squeezes my hand again. "Shh, it's okay," I say smiling. "Don't try to talk. I'm here, baby."

At that he smiles. It's not a full smile, but a half one. Dimple and all.

I can't help it. I start to sob. I sit on the bed and

touch his head. His hair. His face. "I love you. I knew you'd be okay. I—"

I can't talk I'm crying so hard.

Colt's cracked, broken voice silences me. "Danc—er."

My face hurts because I'm smiling so big. "Yes. I want to dance for you," I tell him. It gets me another smile.

His hand slips from mine and I want to cry again, but he just lifts his arm. Touches a strand of my hair, but his arm falls quickly after. "Love . . . you."

Love you. Not just "you too."

It's in those words I know we'll be okay. Everything will be okay.

"I love you too."

EPILOGUE

COLT

Three Months Later

Cheyenne lies beside me in our bed. The apartment is tiny. A studio, but it doesn't fucking matter. What matters is it's ours. And cheap. And Adrian's dumb ass friends aren't partying in our house every night. That matters too. I pull her to me like I do so often now. She still has her room in the dorm because she's supposed to live on campus the first year, but she goes back enough and Andy helps cover for her. The deal works for her because it gives Andy more time with her girl.

"You feel so fucking good." I bury my face in her hair and palm her breast. It feels good to know she's there. That she'll always be there. It's because of her and Adrian I'm even still here. Or not a vegetable. They got me to the hospital quick and from what the docs say, that's what matters.

"Are you ever not horny?" she asks me.

"Why would you ask a crazy question like that, Tiny Dancer?"

She rolls over and faces me. Damn, she's sexy. I can't get over the fact that she's here. That we're fucking here together. I could have died the same day as my mom, which is screwed up, but I didn't. We may have been brought together because of a stupid ass game. Or because we were both screwed up, or needed to change, but we got somewhere important and that's the only thing that counts. I'd play that game over again to be laying here. To know I'm really giving Mom a reason to be proud of me.

"You're right. What could I be thinking?" She laughs and I laugh. I wonder why I didn't do it more often—before her.

"What time do you go to work?" I ask.

"Four. I'm going to hang out with Andy for a little while first."

They've been hanging out a lot lately, which I'm pretty sure Andy is stoked about. She tried to get close to Chey before, but my dancer never really let her. She's getting better at it now.

I lean in and almost kiss her, but know if I do, I won't stop. I never want to stop when I touch her. Most of the time I don't.

"I want to go see Mom before I head out to your aunt and uncle's."

Cheyenne sighs. "You don't have to work yet. They said they'd wait till summer. With your job and school."

I *do* kiss her this time. I pretend it's to shut her up, but it's really because I just like tasting her. She's so familiar now. We know exactly how to move and I've memorized her taste. I'm hard in about two seconds, but really know we don't have time for that.

"They've done a lot for me, Tiny Dancer. I want to pay them off."

They took care of my hospital bills. They paid for Mom to be held until I could be there to tell her goodbye. Her uncle agreed to be my lawyer in my court case, but they ended up dropping the charges since I hadn't had that much weed on me anyway. Of course they also have some stipulations and they want to make sure I'm doing what I'm supposed to do. Not dealing. Being good to Chey. How the hell do you pay someone back for that?

"I know . . . I get it."

"I'm good. No worries." I left school and enrolled part time at the community college. I'm still going, but I'm doing it because I want to be something. Not because I have to, but I also have bills to pay. School's not going anywhere. I can handle doing both.

"No headaches or anything?"

I groan and push out of bed. I know she worries, but it's every day. "No, dear. No headaches. I still know my name, birthday and who you are too. Do you want to go to the doctor with me next time to make sure?"

She gives me a dirty look which tells me I'm being a prick. That's nothing new. It's better, but that's just who I am. I'm lucky she puts up with me . . . but it's not like she's always easy to get along with either. I think that's one of the things that makes us work. I'm glad she stopped bugging me about Gregory though. I hate the motherfucker and don't want to ever hear his name again if I can keep from it. She wasn't happy I didn't want to press charges, but that's not my style. I hate him, but I also know he didn't try to kill me. I pushed him first. Told the cops as much. There's not a whole hell of a lot they could do at that point.

Plus . . . fuck, I'm tired of fighting. Tired of being a quick trigger. That's been my biggest lesson. I need to learn to think before I act.

Greg's daddy pulled him out of school here and that helps too. Knowing he's not around Chey.

"I'm being such a bitch. I can't believe I care about you."

She goes to pout, but I crawl back into bed and straddle her. "I'm glad you care." And I am. We didn't look for this to happen. To fall for each other, but it did and I'm glad. I don't plan on screwing it up.

I take her mouth again, which she gladly lets me.

"Want me to go with you? I have time before I see Andy," she asks.

I nod, knowing exactly what she's asking, and needing her to be with me.

I get up, passing the picture on our bedside table of her mom. It used to be under her mattress. It's cool that she has it up now.

I brush my teeth while she takes a shower. When I put her toothbrush up, I accidentally knock over the bottle for her anxiety meds. It feels pretty full. The good thing is she takes them when she needs them, but it's also good it doesn't happen very often.

We get dressed before heading out to the cemetery. It's cold and even though I know it doesn't make sense I worry about Mom being cold this time of year.

Chey's fingers are laced with mine. I look down at them, again surprised at how we got here. This never would have been me before her. Needing someone. Giving a shit about anyone.

Cheyenne takes the blanket from her other arm and lays it on the ground. We sit and I pull her against me.

I don't really talk to her when I'm here with Chey. It feels weird for some reason, but I talk to Chey. We talk about Mom and I know that if she was here, she'd love to just sit and listen to us. She probably never thought I'd end up with one girl, living with her and willing to admit I love her. Or maybe she did. She always saw stuff in me I wasn't willing to see.

"You can take the car to my aunt and uncle's if

you want," Chey's laying on the blanket with her head in my lap.

"Nah. Adrian's letting me take his. I don't want you without a car."

"Aww. It still shocks me when you're sweet," she teases.

We're both quiet for a few minutes. I look at Mom's headstone. The dates. Her name.

Survived by her son, Colton

Cheyenne's finger traces the word at my wrist.

Mom

"You know . . . I almost felt bad wishing you'd survive."

I look down at her, wondering what she's talking about. Her eyebrows are creased and I smooth them out with my finger, making her laugh. "That doesn't sound real good, Tiny Dancer."

"It was almost guilt . . . because I wanted you with me so much, but I knew if you went, you'd be with her. I was selfish enough to want you with me though."

Her voice sounds so sad. I hate it. We've had enough sadness to last a fucking lifetime. From now on, we should only get the sunshine.

"Come here," I pull her up and she fits in my lap. Her arms wrap around my neck and she buries her face so I can't see her.

"I want to be here with you. I love my mom and I wish like hell she was still here . . . but she's gone. There's no getting her back and . . ." I squeeze her. "You make me want to live. Fuck that. Not just live, you make me want to enjoy it. To fucking love it. I don't pretend anymore. Don't play games anymore."

"The games were more my thing than yours."

I shake my head because we both played them, just in different ways. "She wouldn't have wanted me to go with her." I kiss her head. "I'm right where I belong and where she wanted me to be. Where I want to be . . . With you."

Don't miss Book Two in
The Games Trilogy . . .

FAÇADE

Read on for an exciting sneak preview

CHAPTER ONE

ADRIAN

I didn't sleep for shit last night. Not that I ever really sleep that well, but last night was particularly bad. About one AM I was sick to death of all the drunk, high, loud ass people in my house. Jesus, I wanted them gone. Wanted quiet, normal, but instead I'd smoked another bowl, lied and said I was going to bed before locking myself in my room.

The party went on without me because that's what people do. It's not that they really need me to have fun. I just have the house, shitty as it is, and everyone thinks I'm always down to have a good time. Scratch that. I am always down to have a good time. One look at me shows I'm stoned half the time. Weed? It clouds out the past. Parties drown out the stuff in my head I don't want to hear. But last night of all nights? I deserved to hear that shit, since I'm the one who caused it. So that's what I did. All night. Got blazed out of my head, but kept myself awake so I could think about today.

Around six this morning, I jumped in my car like

I have every January 12th for the past four years and drove my ass here. Rockville, Virginia. Home sweet fucking home except I hate this place with a burning passion. When you spend your childhood getting beat by your dad, all you want to do is escape where you came from. I wouldn't have come if I didn't have to, but after everything, I figure it's the least I can do.

Not that my sister, Angel will ever know I came.

After all this time, I wonder if she'd want me here. If I were her, I wouldn't.

Shaking my thermos, I realize I don't have any more coffee. I toss it onto the passenger side floor and lean back in the seat. Four hours is a long ass time to sit in my car, but I don't want to risk getting out and her seeing me. Probably a good thing I ran out of coffee otherwise I'd have to piss again.

Looking across the street I see all the headstones. Most of them are laid flat so I can't see them from a distance, but I still know exactly which one belongs to Ashton. It's under the big tree. He would have liked that. I bet he would have wanted me to lift him up and put him in that tree if he'd ever had the chance to see it. He thought it was cool to ride on my shoulders. I'd carry him all around the house and he'd laugh like it was fucking Disneyland or something.

Pain grabs hold of me. Threatens to pull me under and for the millionth time, I wonder why I don't let it.

It would be so much easier than walking around in the masks I do now.

"Fuck." I drop my head back. Run a hand through my dark hair. Feel my pocket for the pipe there and wish like hell I could light up. Seems kind of wrong to smoke weed at a cemetery though especially under the circumstances.

I hate the drugs anyway. You wouldn't know it, though. No one does. Adrian's always down to smoke. Adrian's always good for it. That's what everyone thinks, but really I just want to be swept away. To ride a tide or the wind, or whatever the fuck will take me far from here. Weed is the only thing I can find. Sometimes it works, most of the time it doesn't.

My foot itches to push down on the gas pedal, to shove the key in the ignition and get the hell out of here. Not that I ever went real far. I only lived four hours away in Brenton because I couldn't make myself leave the state. But I can't live in Rockville anymore. I don't want to see this. Don't want to be here. I wish I could wake up and find out this has all been some fucked up nightmare. Even if it meant going back in time before Ash and having to deal with shit from my parents.

Leaning forward, I push the useless thermos out of the way and reach for *The Count of Monte Cristo*, which is shoved under the seat. The cover's all old and ripped. The spine's cracked so much from how many times I've read it. It'll probably fall apart any day now.

The thing is, I've always respected Edmond. He went through hell and back, but fought despite it. He didn't fold. He pushed through and worked his ass off to become so much more than he was. He was strong. Not me. I just can't seem to make myself overcome the past.

There's nothing to do but deal with it. And maybe lose myself behind a cloud of smoke or a girl.

I need to turn off my thoughts.

Even though I can't stand hats I grab the one from beside me, push it low on my head, open my book and read. Maybe Edmond can help me clear my head.

Hours later, when I see my sister, Angel, walk over to Ash's grave I don't get out of the car. When some guy walks up and grabs her hand, I don't know who he is and yet, I don't bother finding out. They hug and I don't walk over and do the same thing to her. It's not our thing to stand around having some group mourning session over the two-year-old boy who died too soon.

Nope. This is real life. Not like all the stupid fucking books I read or the movies people watch or the reality shows that couldn't be farther away from reality.

Without moving an inch, I watch her. Watch as she sets flowers on Ashton's grave. As the guy pulls her into a hug. As they kneel on the ground, probably talking to him in a way I'll never have the balls to do.

The guy says something to her and then gets up and walks away. I duck further down in my seat, but no one is paying attention to me. He heads back to a little car and waits.

Angel's hands go to her face and I know she's crying in them. Know she's mourning the loss of Ash, the boy she loved so much. The boy she took care of better than any mom could. I know she sent the guy away because she's like me and needs to handle shit on her own. Only unlike me, she'll never run.

She cries out there for probably thirty minutes. The whole time my chest is tight. Aching. It's hard to breathe and I want to turn away, but I don't. I deserve to feel this way and deserve to see this.

A fist squeezes tighter and tighter around my heart. My face is wet, but I don't bother to wipe away the tears, either. Real men don't fucking cry. That's what dad always said before he hit me in a series of body shots, until I couldn't stop myself from doing just what he said I shouldn't do.

Then he'd beat me harder for being weak.

Angel's shoulders are shaking. I can tell from this far away.

I'm not an idiot. Never have been. I know it wouldn't make me weak to walk over there and hug her. To hold her and tell her it'll be okay, but I still won't do it. What right do I have to try and console her, when I'm the one who destroyed everything?

When I'm the one who let Ash die?

So I sit here and watch her, just so I'll never forget the pain I caused.

headline
ETERNAL

FIND YOUR HEART'S DESIRE...